Breathing
SOCCER

Breathing
SOCCER

DEBBIE SPRING

thistledown press

Library and Archives Canada Cataloguing in Publication

Spring, Debbie, 1953–
Breathing soccer / Debbie Spring.

ISBN 978-1-897235-42-3

I. Title.
PS8587.P734B74 2008   jC813'.6   C2008-900083-8

Cover photograph ©Bob Mitchell/CORBIS
Cover and book design by Jackie Forrie
Printed and bound in Canada

Thistledown Press Ltd.
633 Main Street
Saskatoon, Saskatchewan, S7H 0J8
www.thistledownpress.com

We acknowledge the support of the Canada Council for the Arts, the
Saskatchewan Arts Board, and the Government of Canada through the Book
Publishing Industry Development Program for our publishing program.

Breathing
SOCCER

For Fred, Miriam, Oren, Jasmine, Josh and Patricia.
Thank you for your loving support.

Many thanks to Thistledown Press for believing in me and
for the editorial guidance and wisdom of
R.P. MacIntyre.

1

THE AMBULANCE SIREN ROARED IN MY EARS. White coats surrounded me. A mask covered my mouth.

Who was sitting on me? Why was it so hard to breathe? I flinched as a sharp needle stuck into my arm. Everything got blurry and voices became distant. It took too much effort to understand.

I woke up confused. Where was I? Why was I wearing a hospital gown? Then everything from the night before came flooding back. I remembered the ambulance ride. I rubbed my sore arm where I got a needle.

I peeked through the curtains. A nurse was taking the temperature of a girl, around twelve, my age. She wheezed like a whistle, just like me.

The nurse walked around to my side. I read her nametag, Karen. "Lisa, you're finally awake. The two of you should join a choir — harmonized wheezing."

My roommate giggled, but that only triggered a coughing fit. Nurse Karen opened up the curtain. "Take this puffer, Emily." She handed her a plastic cylinder, the size of a roll of coins with a spout. Emily sprayed its contents into her mouth then held her breath.

"That's better." Nurse Karen tucked her in and took away the puffer.

"Time to wash up, Lisa." She filled a plastic bowl with water and placed it on my tray. "Your hair's short, should be easy to do."

I splashed water on my face.

"What do you know? You have green eyes, underneath those shaggy bangs." Nurse Karen smiled.

"Hazel. That means my eyes change colour."

"The doctor will be in to see you, shortly. I have to go make my rounds. Buzz me, if you need anything."

I pushed away the tray and sank my head into the pillow.

Emily's voice startled me. "Karen's nice, but look out for the other nurse. Zelda is out for blood. Zelda hates kids and she looks after Mutilated Samuel."

"Who's Mutilated Samuel?" I sat up.

"He's this poor kid who had a tragic accident. Samuel lived on a farm and helped in the fields. It's just one of those fluky things. The tractor hit a pothole and Samuel fell and got caught under it. They found the kid, but in pieces. An arm over here, a leg over there."

My skin felt all prickly.

"His father rushed him to the hospital, gushing blood all over the place, carrying what was left of Samuel. His mother ran behind, lugging body parts, a leg, an arm, a hand."

I gasped.

"You know what Zelda, said?"

I held the sheet close up to my face.

"She said, 'Samuel, pull yourself together.' The doctors took hours and sewed poor Samuel back together again, but they couldn't find one of his hands. His mother swore up and down that she brought the hand to the hospital. At night, you better watch out. Samuel's missing hand might walk down the hall and grab you by the throat."

I jumped. "You made that up."

"Ask Nurse Zelda."

No way was I going to ask.

"I dare you to peek into room 333. He's there all right and he's missing a hand. Are you too chicken to look?"

Was I too chicken? I shuddered.

2

"I'M NOT CHICKEN." I CROSSED MY FINGERS. Oh yes, I was. The thought of Samuel's mutilated hand crawling up and grabbing me while I slept was freaking me out. "Okay, I'll check it out . . . later."

There was silence. I stared out the window. It presented a great view of the parking lot. My hospital roommate must have fallen asleep.

"Lisa, you in for asthma?"

I jumped when Emily spoke. I nodded. "Is that what you have?"

"Yeah. Had a doozy of an attack after I visited my friend's house. Didn't know she had a dog until it was too late."

"You react that badly to dogs?" I asked.

Emily nodded.

"That sucks big time. I'd hate to be allergic to dogs. Even if I was, I'd never give up my sheepdog, Shnitzel."

"I had a dog once," Emily's voice cracked. "Snuggles used to sleep in my room and follow me everywhere. When I became allergic, my parents sent him to the Humane Society."

I shivered. He was probably destroyed. Most people only adopt puppies.

Emily lay back on her pillow. "What happened to you?"

"My friend gave me a bite of her egg sandwich. I asked if it had nuts, because I'm allergic. She said no, and since I didn't see any, I ate it. Turned out, there were nuts in the bread. I spit it out right away, but I must have swallowed some because my tongue and throat started to swell and I had trouble breathing. I remember screaming to her mother to inject me with my EpiPen."

"Were you scared?" asked Emily.

"Na," I lied.

"I have an EpiPen too, but I forget what it stands for," said Emily."

"It's a mouthful to say, Epinephrine Auto-Injector," I said.

"Yeah, I know the rest. The needle is filled with adrenaline, and in an emergency, you inject it into your thigh."

I rubbed my sore leg where I got the needle. "I read in the newspaper about a kid who died because the paramedics didn't know she was having an allergic reaction. They gave her oxygen, but it didn't work because the air passage was closed up. Try blowing through a straw when you bend it in half. Nothing gets through."

Emily whistled. "And I thought I was bad."

"Before grade seven, I only had a little wheezing or sometimes a rash. Allergies were never a big deal."

"When did you get an EpiPen?" Emily blew her nose, tooting like a trumpet.

"In the fall, I got tested for allergies and showed four plus for nuts, the worst reaction. That's when the doctor insisted I carry it everywhere. My mother drove me crazy reminding me not to forget it."

"Do you like sports?" Emily asked.

"I'm 'nuts' about soccer."

Emily winced at my pun. "I love playing baseball, but my mother won't let me do anything since getting sick. She treats me like I'm an invalid."

Emily kept talking but I didn't want to listen any more. My head pounded so I squeezed my eyes closed. She finally figured I had fallen asleep and read her book.

Will my mother stop me from playing soccer? I worried.

3

Nurse Karen came back in. "Lisa, your parents and Dr. Emerson are here to see you."

Drumming up the courage I asked, "What room am I in?"

"You are in room 331," said Nurse Karen.

Mutilated Samuel is right next door. The hand. I shivered. What if the hand goes looking for Samuel and finds me by mistake?

Dr. Emerson walked in with my parents. He's always been our family doctor.

"You gave your parents quite a scare," said Dr. Emerson.

I managed a nod.

My parents stood around the bed. They both looked exhausted with puffy eyes and slumped shoulders.

"Can't take any more chances," said the doctor.

I raised my hand in a scout's honour pledge. "I promise to carry my EpiPen all the time."

"That's not all there is to it, Lisa. You need an asthma puffer. Take it whenever you have an asthma attack. No trading food, and eat only what your mother sends you."

I stared at the moving mouth and pretended a fly darted in.

The doctor rattled on. "Always read labels. Don't take someone's word that there aren't any nuts in it. Are you listening?"

"Yes, Dr. Emerson."

"Running induces asthma. No more gym. Cold air gives you asthma. No more recess or playing outside. I'll write you a note to excuse you."

No more gym, no more playing outside! My head was pounding. They've put me in jail and thrown away the key.

The doctor left. My parents stayed, but I stopped talking and kept yawning 'till everyone left. Turning on the television, just my luck, I only got three channels — and they all showed the news.

"Disaster struck rower Silken Laumann. Canada's Olympic hopeful for the 1992 Summer Olympics in Barcelona Spain, has been seriously injured and it might be the end of her career," said the announcer. I turned up the volume and watched Laumann rowing in single sculls.

As the announcer continued, there was a news clip of Laumann being carried off on a stretcher. "Just ten weeks before the Olympics, Silken has been in a boating accident during practice for a regatta in Essen, Germany. A competitor's boat collided with hers causing severe injuries including a broken leg, a severed muscle and damaged nerves. Splinters of wood are imbedded throughout the wound.

There was a close-up of Laumann proudly standing at attention while the Canadian flag raised and the Canadian anthem played. "Laumann, 1991 world champion in singles, was considered almost a certainty for the Olympic title until now," said the announcer.

"We are standing at Laumann's hospital bed. She is recovering from leg surgery. Silken, tell us how you feel."

"The lower leg looks like a small shark took a bite out of it. The surgeon here in Germany told me to forget the Olympics," said Silken showing her bandaged leg.

The announcer again stood outside the hospital. "It will probably conclude her career in sports. She's scheduled for her sixth operation later this month to complete the repair job on her right leg."

I'm not the only one with problems. Poor Silken Laumann.

I switched off the television and closed my eyes. A hand crawled up and grabbed my throat. I woke up wheezing.

4

I LOOKED AT THE CALENDAR. ONLY TWO WEEKS since my life sentence. Seems like forever. I pressed my nose against the window and watched my friends laughing and playing soccer during recess. A tear rolled down my face and I wiped it with my sleeve. It's not fair. I pounded the windowsill.

The bell rang and I waited by the door for my two best friends Janis and Nancy. Janis comes up to Nancy's and my shoulders and her blonde bangs always fall in her eyes — same as my sheepdog. Nancy has shocking red, curly hair. Because I was dying for company, my mouth fell open as Janis and Nancy walked right by me into the classroom. A lump formed in my throat as I took my seat. I twisted a strand of my frizzy hair around my finger.

Mrs. Taylor told us to work in groups for our history project.

With hesitation, I went over to Nancy. "Want to be partners?"

Nancy cleared her throat. "Can't. I promised Janis."

"Three's okay."

"We've got too many already. Linda and Arla are in with us too."

"Oh." I knew what was happening. I wasn't one of the gang any more. I shuffled off on my own. For the next forty minutes, I stared at the book without reading a single word.

The second the 3:30 bell rang, we stampeded for the lockers where Janis was handing out birthday invitations.

Nancy read her invitation out loud. "Come to my sleepover-soccer party." She hugged Janis. "You bet I'll come."

I rushed over. "Can I play right defence?"

Janis frowned. "I'd invite you, Lisa, only Nancy's mother told my mother everything about having to give you a shot with your needle thing. She nearly had a heart attack doing it. My mother's too scared to have you over, you know, in case you get sick."

"Tell her not to worry."

"Well, you know my mother, once she says no, she means no." Janis shrugged.

"Yeah, I know." I hurried off. It's like I have a disease and everybody's afraid they'll catch it.

I ran all the way home, wheezing loudly.

"Good Lord, just listen to you." Mom spilled her coffee onto our white carpet. Grabbing a rag, she got down on her hands and knees to blot the brown spot.

Shnitzel jumped and knocked me over, licking me on the face. I laughed and wrestled with him. Mom stood over me glaring. I rolled away from Shnitzel and got him a doggie bone, which he gnawed on greedily.

"I'm driving you from now on."

"I'm fine," I argued. "It's only a ten-minute walk. The kids will make fun of me if you drive. They'll call me a baby."

"Go take your spray."

Slowly, I exhaled. Then I put my lips around the puffer, inhaling as I pushed down on the end. The medication sprayed into my mouth and I held my breath. My breathing returned to normal.

My dumb, ten-year-old sister grabbed a cookie then ran outside to shoot some baskets on our driveway. All the relatives say that Sharon is the spitting image of me, just a smaller version. That's an insult because I think she's ugly. If Sharon was allowed to play outside, then I was going to play outside too and nothing was going to stop me. So, I challenged my mother. "I'm going out to kick the ball around."

"Oh no, you're not. You'll get an attack." Mom stood blocking the way.

I ran up to my room and slammed the door. I pounded my fist into my pillow and let the tears flow. Shnitzel whined and scratched outside my door. Sniffing, I let him in. Sensing that I was sad, he cuddled in my lap, licking the tears from my face.

Now what was I going to do?

5

It was hard to get up for school in the morning. At breakfast, I tried one last time. "I'm walking," I declared.

"No you're not. Doctor's orders," Mom insisted.

I got into the car for the five-minute ride. Janis and Nancy were knocking a ball back and forth between them. They saw me get out of the car and looked at me with pity.

I felt stupid standing there, so I ran and joined them. Nancy headed the ball towards Janis but I intercepted and kicked it back to Nancy. We ignored the first bell. At the second bell, we raced to line up.

My chest felt heavy and my breathing sounded raspy. All eyes turned on me. My face felt hot and flushed. I felt like a freak. Maybe if I held my breath. That only sent me into a coughing spasm. Reluctantly, I reached into my pocket and grabbed my puffer. I sprayed it into my mouth. As the mob of kids moved in, my thoughts jumped around my head. The kids were whispering about me. I was an outcast.

That night, I dreamt that an elephant sat on my chest and I couldn't breathe. I woke up, gasping. In the dark, I groped for my puffer, knocking my water glass over. I took it once, then twice when the wheezing persisted. It still didn't work. I felt like someone was holding a pillow over my face. I was suffocating.

Dr. Emerson warned me, no more than two puffs or I might overdose. Panic-stricken, I woke up my parents who drove me to the hospital in their pyjamas.

We had to wait two hours. I always wanted to stay up until the sun rose. I thought that would be so grown up. The middle of the night wasn't so exciting. In the emergency waiting room, there was a middle-aged woman with a cut on her forehead, a man with a beard holding his arm funny, a couple who took turns trying to calm a crying baby, and other sad-looking people. Not my idea of a good time.

Finally, a nurse called my name and ushered me into a tiny room. The doctor examined me and gave me adrenaline, oxygen and antihistamine.

Then I was admitted into a semi-private room because of my father's insurance policy. My parents kissed me on the cheek and left me. They looked so tired and worn that I wished that I could have gotten a bed for them to get some shut-eye. I knew that my father would drop my mother off at home and then have only enough time to grab some breakfast before going to work. I felt really guilty.

A girl slept in the other bed. Tears welled up in my eyes. I used to have allergies but it was no big deal. Now I breathed unevenly through the oxygen mask.

Early the next morning, I turned on the television low and again nothing but the news was on.

"Silken Laumann shocked the public when she announced that she is still going to compete in the 1992 Summer Olympics. She already is training in her hospital bed."

Wow! Silken Laumann's tough. Drumming up all the will power that I had, I did ten sit-ups before collapsing on the bed. The oxygen mask hid my smile.

6

Stiffly, I got up to go to the bathroom. I glanced at the name, Alice, posted on my roommate's bed. Alice winked. I was surprised at how strong and normal she looked.

In the washroom, I took a long hard look at myself. Staring back at me was not the tanned, healthy, young face that I had known, but some stranger. My complexion was pasty, my eyes puffy and I had lost weight. I looked scrawny. What happened to my muscles? Slowly, I made my way back to bed with Alice watching me. "Staring problems?" I challenged.

"Curious, that's all," said Alice.

"You look too healthy to be in here."

"I'm out of here." Alice pulled on her white shorts. "Had a big attack last night when there was too much smoke at the restaurant."

"Ask for non-smoking."

"Did, but they put the non-smoking tables right beside the smoking section. Zapped me good. Won't go there again." Alice looked at her watch. "Hurry up, Dad." She tapped her foot.

"What's the rush?" I asked.

"Got a tennis match in half an hour."

My eyes went wide. "How can you play?"

"Follow through like this." Alice mimed hitting the ball.

"Very funny. Doesn't exercise give you problems?" I asked.

"Sure. But I just take my spray before I play."

"And your doctor allows that?" My eyes went wide.

"Why not?" asked Alice.

"My doctor won't."

Alice shrugged. "Change doctors."

"Can I have the name of your doctor?"

"Dr. Bellows. She treats a lot of asthmatic athletes."

"But my doctor said, 'no exercise'."

"Your doctor's from the Middle Ages. Of course, you can do everything. What's your game?" asked Alice.

"Soccer."

"Just take your spray before playing. As I said, no big deal."

No big deal. The words echoed in my head.

Alice grabbed a piece of paper and scribbled down Dr. Bellows name. "Here, go see her and get a life."

Alice's father came and we said our goodbyes. I sat there stunned, clutching my piece of paper. My eyes started to get heavy. I felt a cold chill running down my back.

That's when I saw Mutilated Samuel's hand walking down the hallway stopping in front of my room. "Not in here," I cried. I gasped as the hand walked on fingertips straight into my room. It tapped its fingers and headed straight for my bed. I pulled up the bed sheet to my chin, quivering. Then it climbed the sheet and walked across my body. The hand grabbed my throat and started strangling me. I clutched at the hand and we wrestled. It was winning. As I grew weaker, my eyes bulged.

I bolted up in bed. Sweat poured down my face. I was alone in my room. Then a lady with a blue, paper hair-cap brought in dinner. Famished, I uncovered the tray. I gagged. It was tongue. Did it belong to Mutilated Samuel too? First the hand, now his tongue? Fighting nausea, I quickly covered the tray and pushed it far away. I lay back onto my pillow.

7

Back home again, I argued with my mom. "I have to see Dr. Bellows." Shnitzel had his ball in his mouth and he dropped it at my feet. "Mom, he wants to go out."

"I don't need another midnight visit to the hospital. Neither of you are going outside. He'll just have to wait until your father gets home because he's too big for Sharon to handle."

"Can't I play ball with him, just for a few minutes?" Shnitzel kept scratching at the door and whining.

"No, means no." Shnitzel heard the tone in Mom's voice and hid under the table. "Shnitzel will have to learn the new rules, the same as you. Besides, what's wrong with Dr. Emerson? He's been our family doctor since you were born."

"I want a second opinion. If you don't take me, I'll go myself."

Mom wavered. "It's that important to you?"

"It is."

"I'll discuss this with your father."

There was no use arguing. I would have to wait and see. If my father said no, then I would have to somehow convince him that Dr. Bellows was my only hope. I know I can do things. I'm still the same kid I was before all of these attacks, aren't I?

The next morning, Dad drove me to school. Here was my big chance to convince him. "Did Mom talk to you about me going to Dr. Bellows?" I asked.

"Yes, she did." Dad changed the radio from my favourite rock station to a classical station.

"And?" I asked.

"And, I don't see anything wrong with the doctor we have been using since you were born."

"I just want a second opinion. She specializes in allergies."

"She does, eh?"

"Yes! Can we Dad?"

"Okay, fine. But you have to listen to the doctor's advice. And no more fighting with your mother about what you can or can't do, okay?"

"That's fair," I said.

We arrived at school and I waved goodbye to my father feeling on top of the world. Dad said, yes. Dr. Bellows will allow me to play outside and to play soccer. I know she will.

All my friends were standing around talking about Janis's birthday party, the party that I wasn't invited to. She used to be my best friend. This all didn't seem real. Why was my life being taken away from me? My lip quivered and I fought to hold it in. I couldn't let them see me cry.

"At Janis's party, I want Arla to be on my team," Nancy announced. "She is an awesome mid-fielder."

"I want to play goalie," Linda butted in.

Taking a deep breath, I joined them. "Let me play defence at the party. I've got to practise for tryouts."

Everybody stopped talking. Janis looked at me kind of funny.

Embarrassed, I walked away.

Later, at my desk, I pretended that I had work to do, but all I did was doodle in my notebook. Anything to try and look busy. I felt as if I was being shunned, as if I was a religious outcast where the person continues to live in the community but becomes like a ghost. People aren't allowed to talk to her, and they treat her like she is invisible.

Fed up, I shoved my notebook aside. Nobody's going to kick me around, I muttered. The second Mrs. Taylor left the room for the office, I went over to Nancy's desk.

"Want to come over after school?" I held my breath.

8

"COME OVER. IT WILL BE FUN," I said.

Nancy shifted from one foot to the other. "Um," she hesitated.

I crossed my fingers. "Remember the time when we baked a cake and put salt in by mistake instead of sugar?"

"Yeah, it was gross." Nancy laughed. "Okay, I guess I can come over for a little while."

I sighed deeply. Things weren't quite back to normal, but it was a start. I gave Nancy a piece of gum. She slipped off her friendship bracelet and put it on my wrist. That meant a lot to me.

After school, Mom picked Nancy and me up even though it was a gorgeous, warm, spring day.

"Did you phone Dr. Bellows?" I asked, anxiously.

"Yes."

"And?"

"His secretary said that you need a referral from Dr. Emerson, so I looked after that. But Dr. Bellows is booked solid for two weeks."

"Two weeks?"

"You don't know how lucky you are. Normally, you have to wait a few months to see a specialist. I just called right after a patient cancelled, so the secretary was able to fit you in."

That's cutting it close to soccer tryouts."

"You're not allowed," Mom reminded me.

"Dr. Bellows will let me. You'll see."

Mom shook her head. "Don't get your hopes up."

Nancy pretended to study her nails.

Shnitzel put his paws on my legs. We wrestled. At least he treated me like he always did. His big tongue licked my face and I gave him a doggie biscuit.

Nancy and I had a snack of cheese and crackers. Then we went to my room and looked at *Young Teen* magazine. We studied the clothes and make-up trying to pick up all the pointers. I liked the article, "Should Girls Beat Boys In Sports?" Some girls said no, some yes. I said definitely yes.

Lying on my tummy, leaning on my elbows, I sighed. This was like old times.

Sharon ran in holding her soccer ball. "There's a game going on at the park."

Nancy jumped up. "All right! Let's go."

"Everybody's practising for soccer tryouts. I'll be on the junior team. I'll finally be out of Peewee." Sharon ran out.

"Come on, Lisa." I didn't move. Nancy stopped short. "Oh, yeah, you can't play outside."

It was as if a sledgehammer hit me over the head.

"I forgot you're not allowed outside. It's okay, we can play in here." Nancy sat down twiddling her thumbs.

"How about cards?" I asked, in a tight voice.

"Sure. Let's play Crazy Eights."

I dealt the cards. Nancy lost the first two games because she kept checking her watch and staring out the window.

"I better go home and help my mother make dinner. See you," Nancy called as she rushed out the door.

"Bye." She sure was in a hurry to leave. Never in a million years would she volunteer to help make supper and I knew how much she hated being inside on such a great day. Who would want to miss a game of soccer to play with an invalid? Things had changed. I never again wanted to have friends over. I closed the door after Nancy like I closed the door on my old life.

Shnitzel nuzzled me with his black, cold nose and I patted him. Shnitzel understood, but nobody else did.

9

"THIS IS RIDICULOUS," MOM COMPLAINED. "WE NEVER had to wait so long in Dr. Emerson's office."

"She's a specialist, Mom. Most good specialists are busy."

"She? Dr. Bellows is a woman? I just assumed . . . " Mom stammered.

"Welcome to the twentieth century, Mom."

Bored, I went to look at the framed newspaper clippings up on the wall. "Renn Crichlow is the first Canadian to win a world championship in Paris of 1991. He has risen to the top of the kayaking sport despite problems with asthma. Crichlow is driven by a desire to test his limits." He won the Worlds with asthma? Pretty impressive, I thought.

I read on. "His average day of training at his home base in Burnaby, British Columbia, is heavy. Weight training at 7 AM for two hours, classes at Simon Fraser University for a few hours, swim two-thousand to six-thousand metres, train in the boat for two hours, homework and bed."

The article continued, "You stand on the podium and you hear the anthem and you think of all the mornings and all the rainy days and all the times you were sick and you think, 'This is worth it'."

Wow. He has asthma just like me, and look what he's accomplished.

Another half hour ticked by. "Lisa Jacobs," the receptionist called. I jumped up. "Follow me." Mom came too.

Mom looked Dr. Bellows over. "You're very young."

"Thank you, Mrs. Jacobs."

I blushed. I'm sure she knew that my mother meant it as a put down.

Dr. Bellows asked for my medical and family history. Mom rattled off the times she could remember that I had allergic reactions. Then the doctor examined me.

I was sweating bricks. Will she let me play soccer? What if she doesn't?

Dr. Bellows had me breathe into a machine.

"Is this really necessary?" asked my mother in a condescending voice.

"Absolutely. I need to measure Lisa's breath control and volume. These tests are how we measure allergies. What I want to do next is a scratch test. There are four categories of testing: food, animals, medications and environmental. The skin pricks are done on the inside of the forearm. When there is a positive reaction to a tested substance, the skin around the prick point becomes itchy and then red and swollen. The reactions vary from 1 to 4, with 4 being the biggest reaction. These results occur within fifteen to twenty minutes. My nurse will mark down Lisa's reactions."

Dr. Bellows spoke into the intercom. "Ricky, can you come in and help with the allergy tests?"

A large man walked in. He looked like a wrestler.

My mouth fell open. "You're a nurse?"

10

THE LARGE MAN WITH HAIRY ARMS LAUGHED. "Most people expect Florence Nightingale. Many nursing jobs require lifting people so they need someone with a little muscle. I'm also a softy." He winked. "I love the soaps."

Even my mother laughed.

Dr. Bellows started the scratch test. Ricky jotted down the results.

"One plus for spinach," said Dr. Bellows.

"Aw. Why can't spinach be higher," I complained.

"Three plus for potatoes," said Dr. Bellows.

"But I love fries," I complained.

"There is no justice," said the nurse.

After about ten different scratches, I started to get red marks on my arm. "My arm itches and I want to scratch it. Is that why you call it a scratch test?" I joked.

"That's a good one," said Dr. Bellows.

When the tests were done, Dr. Bellows went over the results. "Lisa, you're allergic to dust, pollen, ragweed, grass, potatoes, liver . . . "

"Liver? Great."

"I thought you might like that one." Dr. Bellows continued reading. "Of course, nuts. That one you already know. Right Lisa?"

I nodded.

"Feathers, hay, all spice, nutmeg, cats, dogs."

"Dogs!" I felt all the blood drain from my face.

Dr. Bellows looked at me. "Do you have a dog?"

"Yes."

"I'm sorry, but the dog will have to go."

"Not Shnitzel!" I cried.

"I know this is hard, but your dog is making your immune system fight too hard. Your reactions to everything are getting worse."

I just made the biggest mistake of my life seeing this new doctor. My dog was my best friend. He was there to greet me when I came home. He was there to sit on my lap and lick me when I was down. Nobody was taking my dog away. Nobody.

11

Mom clenched her hands. "How will I ever remember the list?"

"Don't worry, Ricky will give you a copy. And here are instructions, Mrs. Jacobs, on how to clean your house."

"I already know how to clean my house thank you very much," Mom said, crisply.

"Do you use all purpose cleaners?"

"Yes."

"They give Lisa asthma. Start using water and vinegar, baking soda instead of all-purpose cleaners, and substitute lemon juice and oil for wood. Lisa needs to take a cortisone spray — a puffer — to help prevent future asthma attacks. She should rinse out her mouth afterwards. And Lisa, take this other spray, before exercise. That will help ward off an attack."

Did she say before exercise? But did that mean soccer? The reactions of all the tests left me feeling sick. I was bursting to ask the doctor if I could go back to soccer. My mouth opened then closed. What if she says no?

"You look like you're dying to say something."

"Can I play outside?"

"Of course."

"Can I take gym?"

"Absolutely."

"What about soccer?" I held my breath.

"Go ahead."

"You are a normal child, Lisa. Just remember that. The only difference is that you have to take medications."

I swallowed hard.

"I'm going to teach you how to breathe properly. It's the same breathing that actors use to project their voices to the last row so that they can be heard. An Olympic athlete uses this technique to have endurance. Breathe deeply from the stomach, not the chest. Put one hand on your stomach; push it out like a balloon. Place your hands on your shoulders. Did your shoulders rise?"

I nodded, yes.

"That means your breathing is shallow. Push out with your stomach. Try again." I breathed deeply.

"Now you've got it."

I beamed.

"When you get an attack, sit out for a few minutes and slow down your breathing. Just relax. The more uptight you get, the shallower your breathing gets. You need to build up your lungs, Lisa. Go get more exercise and fresh air."

I smiled from ear to ear.

Mom looked sheepish. "I guess I have a lot to learn. Thank you, Doctor. We've been in here for a long time. We should let you see your other patients."

"I give each patient all the time that he or she needs. In the first visit, it's necessary to do all the tests. Lisa needs to work at everything I told her. Make an appointment for next month as a follow-up. She won't have to be in here as long."

"Bye, Dr. Bellows." I waved.

"Call me if you have any more questions."

We walked out into the waiting room. The secretary called in the next patient. "Renn Crichlow."

My mouth gaped open. I stared. A huge, really well built man stood up. His arms were so muscular. "Are you Renn Crichlow?" I asked, in wonder.

"That's right."

"Can I have your autograph?"

"Got a pen?" Renn smiled.

The secretary gave me a pen and paper.

"What's your name?"

"Lisa."

"Do you like sports?"

"Soccer."

"You got asthma?"

I nodded, yes.

"Me too." Renn winked at me and signed his autograph.

I stood there stunned as Renn went into Dr. Bellows' office.

In the car, I read the note. "To Lisa, Champions Never Give Up." I re-read the words over and over.

I was going to play soccer. One day, I would be a champion! Let the training begin.

12

Every morning, I did one hundred push-ups, one hundred sit-ups and one hundred stride-jumps. Sweat poured down my face. I was up to eighty stride-jumps and my calves burned. Got to get in shape fast, I puffed. Tryouts soon. Finally I hit one hundred and collapsed on the floor, gasping. I hurried downstairs and blended an energy milkshake with milk, banana and yogurt. Then I jogged to school. If Silken Laumann could train hard, so could I.

The kids acted surprised to see me playing soccer with them. We waited until the second bell and then made a dash for class.

Janis cupped her hands at her mouth and shouted, "Hey Lisa, practice after school at my place."

"You bet," I answered.

In class, Mrs. Taylor handed out freshly copied pages. I sniffed my paper. Big mistake. The odour from the printing chemicals brought on an asthma attack. Stifling a cough, I raised my hand. "May I be excused?"

Mrs. Taylor gave me permission.

In the washroom, I practised the breathing exercises that Dr. Bellows taught me. The mirror reflected my surprised expression as my asthma went away. I didn't even need my puffer, I realized. When I got back to class, nobody knew about my attack. Good, I didn't want to be treated like a freak.

After school, Nancy, Janis and I practised soccer in Janis's backyard. It bugged me how Janis's mother kept checking on me.

"What gives with your mother?" I asked.

Janis looked down at her shoes. "She's worried that you'll have an asthma attack here."

"If I do, I'll just take my puffer."

"She thinks you're going to die on her."

"She's right. I'm going to croak."

"What?" Janis's eyes went wide.

"Everybody dies," I said, smugly.

Janis punched me in the arm. "Let's play soccer."

We kicked the ball up and down the yard. My breathing got laboured so I sat out for a minute and practised my breathing exercises. It helped a little, but not completely.

Janis's mother ran out waving her arms. "Quick, call the doctor."

"Why?" I asked.

"You're having an attack."

"So?"

"What do you mean, 'so'?" Her voice was shrill.

"Don't you ever get out of breath?"

"Yes, but . . . "

"You're out of breath now," I pointed out.

"What does that have to do with anything?"

"It's no big deal. The only difference is I take my puffer." I squirted my inhaler into my mouth and held my breath for as long as I could so that the medicine wouldn't get exhaled. Then I winked at Janis's mother and rejoined the game. She just stood there not knowing what to do.

Later that evening, I went through our newspapers and magazines. Carefully, I cut out every picture and article on Silken Laumann and put them into my scrapbook.

The next day, workers arrived at my place. They tore out the rug in my room. I hated to see my rug go, but Dr. Bellows said that it collected too much dust and dust mites. I guess I could live with that - or without it. But I couldn't live with losing Shnitzel.

13

SHNITZEL GROWLED AT THE WORKERS SO I had to take him into the den. I held Shnitzel on my lap and stroked him. "We found a great home for you." I swallowed hard. "Aunt Irene and Uncle Ray are terrific. You'll love it there because they live on a farm. You can run around chasing mice and gophers and you can even visit the horses." Tears flowed down my face. "I wish you didn't have to go. I'll visit, I promise."

Sharon burst into the room. "I hate you. It's all your fault Shnitzel has to leave." She slammed the door behind her.

Shnitzel whined. "I'm sorry Shnitzel." I buried my face in his fur. Even though I got pins and needles in my legs, I wouldn't let go of Shnitzel, even when the workers left.

Mom came in with downcast eyes. "It's time."

"Can I come?" I asked.

"It would be easier if you said your goodbyes now."

I hugged Shnitzel and watched as my sheepdog jumped into the car wagging his tail. Stupid dog. Thinks he's only going for a car ride.

I stood there watching the car move further and further away. I just lost my best friend. I walked back into the house like I was walking down death row.

I could hear Sharon screaming. "I hate you, Lisa. I hate you."

I felt miserable. I knew if Shnitzel had to go because of Sharon's allergies, I would never forgive her. So why should she forgive me?

14

Every room reminded me of Shnitzel. There by the television was his favourite spot to curl up in, and in the corner was some of his shed fur. By the back door was a chewed-up tennis ball. Everywhere I looked, I saw him. I couldn't take it any longer so I went for a walk in the park. But that was worse because so many people were out walking their dogs, throwing sticks, balls or Frisbees with them, and patting them. Dogs, dogs everywhere. Then I saw a sheepdog. "Shnitzel," I thought. But as I got closer, I saw that he wasn't as big and shaggy as my dog. My dog. I no longer had a dog.

Slowly, I walked home. When I entered, Sharon's eyes were red from crying and she glared at me.

I turned on the television and channel surfed. I heard Mom come through the front door and a few minutes later into the den. She had met my uncle halfway and he had taken Shnitzel the rest of the way to his farm. Mom looked exhausted from the long drive.

"Are you all right?" Mom asked me.

"How can I be all right?" I snapped and I ran to my room.

Dad tried too hard to be cheerful. He was an insurance salesman and knew how to win people over. "I brought you a new computer game," he said. "Your favourite."

And it was too. I pushed it aside. "It won't replace Shnitzel."

"I know, honey." He tried to hug me, but I pulled away. He left the room looking dejected.

Mom tried to coax me down all evening and finally gave up and left a tray of food. If I ate, I would throw up. Eventually, I tried playing the new computer game, just to take my mind off Shnitzel, but it didn't work. I couldn't concentrate and each time I was knocked out at level one. Finally, I just went to bed and endlessly counted sheep. Is Shnitzel missing me with new people and a new home or is he too busy sniffing out the barn and chasing small animals? Has he forgotten me already?

In the middle of the night, I had another bad asthma attack so I tried slowing down my breathing and taking my sprays, but nothing worked. Reluctantly, I woke up my parents.

"We're going to the hospital," my mother declared.

My father put both legs into a single pant leg and nearly fell on his face.

"Wait," I insisted. "Call Dr. Bellows first. She gave us an emergency number."

Dr. Bellows explained to my father how to make me a steam tent. My father took me downstairs where he draped sheets over the kitchen table and put the kettle on underneath. I sat under the tent inhaling the steam. My breathing calmed down and slowly became normal.

Before I knew it, I was back in my own bed. I needed my sleep because the tryouts were tomorrow. I just had to make the team.

15

In the morning, I felt sluggish and tired from the night's ordeal. I dragged myself down to breakfast and by habit went to fill Shnitzel's food dish. The dish was gone from the corner. Then it hit me like a cold shower. Schnitzel was gone for good. I fought back the tears.

Sharon glared daggers at me. "Hope you don't make the team."

"Sharon," Mom scolded. "How could you?"

"I mean it."

Mom sent Sharon to her room and she ran out knocking down her chair.

Great. Now Sharon hated me even more, if that was humanly possible. Her tryouts were in the afternoon and I hoped that she made the junior team or she would blame me for that, too.

"Hurry up, Lisa or you'll be late." Dad looked up from his paper sipping his coffee.

I could hardly eat, because I had a lump in my throat, but I forced myself to have something. I needed energy to play, I reminded myself. Before leaving, I remembered to take my puffer.

The field was crowded with parents and children. Every kid was eager to make the team. The coach handed out bibs with numbers on them. I was number thirteen. Lucky me, I thought.

The drills started. I had to dribble the ball around each of the orange pylons. Then the coach threw the ball at my head and I headed it back to him. I felt like a goat butting heads. Next, I kicked ten balls at the goalie, but only six went in. Then I bounced the ball from one knee to the other. Every exercise was timed.

We played a short practise game while the coach took notes. I played defence and stopped every ball that came to my side. I covered so that nothing could get past me and I gave clean, hard passes. During halftime, my puffer fell out of my pocket and I saw Coach Wilcox staring at me with a funny expression on his face.

After the tryouts, the results were tacked to a tree. Anybody with fifteen out of twenty got on the team. I skimmed the paper for my name. "Yippee!" I cried. Seventeen points. I waited anxiously for my interview.

"Jacobs," Coach Wilcox called.

I jumped up and ran over.

Coach Wilcox sat on a lawn chair. "Congratulations, Lisa, you're on the team."

I grinned. "Can I play right defence?"

"Actually," Coach Wilcox cleared his throat, "I put you down as a sub."

"A sub!" I exclaimed. That means I only play if someone's away or gets hurt during the game. But I got seventeen points. Other girls on the team only scored fifteen and they're not subs, I thought.

"You did great, kid."

"Then why a sub?"

"I'll be honest kid: You could get sick on me. I read the medical form that your parents filled out." Every player needed one in order to play in the league.

"I won't get sick, I promise." I tried to explain. "If I take my puffer . . . "

Coach Wilcox interrupted. "It's not your fault, kid. That's just the way it goes."

"But . . . "

"That's final." He called out the next name.

I walked away in a hopeless daze.

16

It was late Sunday morning when Dad came into my bedroom. "Are you going to stay in bed all day?"

"What's to get up for?"

"You've got a soccer game in an hour."

"Who cares?"

"One of the players might be sick or too tired and the coach will put you on."

"I doubt it."

"It's bound to happen. The coach will see how good you are and then he'll want to keep you in."

I swung my legs over the bed. "Fine, I'll give it a try."

"That's my girl." My father puffed on his cigarette.

"Dad, smoke gives me asthma. Can you give it up for me?"

Dad looked down at his shoes. "I've tried to quit three times, honey, but I can't."

"You stand there telling me I can do something while you turn around and tell me you can't."

Dad hung his head as he left my room.

I put on my yellow soccer outfit that read Appliance Reliance. Teams were always named after their sponsor. Why couldn't we have a cool name like Yellow Hornets?

When I got into the car, Sharon was already in the front seat wearing her orange jersey that said, Plumber Joe. I guess my team name wasn't so bad after all.

"I love playing mid-fielder," she bragged. "Too bad, you can't play."

I felt like slugging her. I put on my earphones and tuned her out.

Later, at the game, Appliance Reliance was ahead 3-0. "Go yellow, go," I cheered. The purple team looked tired and sluggish as we ran circles around them. I watched by the sidelines. At halftime, I ran to the coach. "Can I go on?"

"Not yet, kid." He called out, "Lily, take left defence."

I sat back down. Fifteen minutes later, my team was ahead two more points. What a slaughter. The whistle blew for substitution. "Coach, we're creaming them. You can afford to take a chance with me."

"Samantha take right defence," Coach Wilcox commanded.

"I'm too tired, Coach. I've been off only five minutes the whole game. Send Lisa in. She hasn't played yet." Sweat poured down Samantha's face.

"I make the calls around here. Don't be a wimp, Samantha. Get in there."

Samantha shrugged and ran in. I sat back down.

When the game ended, Lily and Samantha jumped up and down. "We creamed them," Samantha cried.

I didn't feel elated because I didn't feel part of the team. I went up to the coach. "Will I play next game?"

"We'll see."

"That means no," I muttered. I walked away from the team, not my team because I wasn't a part of it and I walked away from the sport that I loved. I walked away from all hope.

17

I WAS QUIET IN THE CAR RIDE HOME. Sharon wouldn't shut up, bragging about all of her amazing passes. Dad tried to jolly me out of my bad mood. "How about some ice cream?"

"Yeah," cried Sharon.

"No, thanks," I said.

"Want me to pick up a video?" asked Dad.

"I'm not in the mood. I just want to go home," I said.

"I want ice cream and I want a movie," said Sharon.

Dad lit a cigarette and drove on in silence heading home.

"No fair," sulked Sharon.

I stayed in my room the rest of the afternoon, staring out the window. Look at all the parents dropping their kids off for Janis's birthday party. A party I should have been at. After my showdown with Janis's mother, she was even more determined not to have me over again. Janis told me that she pleaded with her until she was blue in the face, but her mother wouldn't budge. She was convinced that I would have another asthma attack on her property and either sue her or die. I guess I had just made things worse.

There was Nancy carrying a present and her soccer ball. At that moment, Nancy looked up at my window and I ducked. I hoped she hadn't seen me. Tears fell down my face as I closed the window to drown out the laughter. The hours ticked slowly by.

Monday morning, I stood at my locker pretending I was busy getting books while I listened to the chatter of my friends talking about the soccer party.

"What a save Penny made," said Janis.

"Thanks," said Penny. "Did you see that kick Nancy did? Right into the next yard." I walked away. I was no longer a part of it. I was an outsider again.

At lunchtime, feeling sorry for myself, I sat by myself. There wasn't much else to do but pour myself into my work. If I looked busy, then it wasn't as embarrassing eating alone. I watched as my classmates mimicked my teachers and laughed their heads off.

I threw my lunch into the garbage. I had lost my appetite. Life couldn't get much worse.

The boys were horsing around and all of a sudden, I was wearing Nathan's lunch of hotdog and fries. Ketchup and mustard stained my new white blouse. The boys snorted and laughed while the girls giggled. I ran to the bathroom and tried to blot out the stains, but I only made things worse. Now my blouse was blotchy with yellow and red and soaking wet. Why do I always make things worse?

18

For some stupid reason, I thought if I didn't show up all week at soccer practice and the game, then the coach would miss me and call me to play. Nobody called. Nobody cared. Sharon found out that we won again. It was pretty obvious the team didn't need me. This wasn't any fun. The sky was too blue and I was too restless. I paced back and forth. I couldn't stand being cooped up in my room another minute.

I flipped through my scrapbook and read about Silken Laumann and how hard she was training. How could I make the coach notice me? Maybe I could go to all the practices and prove that I was worth putting in the game. I'd practise everyday after school too. It'd be better than staying in my room. During practice, everybody got to play. Beth was the other sub besides me. Her problem was her shape — like an apple, short and chunky.

I got off my butt and went to practice.

Beth approached me. "Where you been?"

"No place special." I shrugged.

"You missed all last week."

"Didn't think anyone would notice." I kicked the dirt.

"Why do you say that?"

"Did the coach let you play?" I chided.

"No, but . . . "

"That's why I didn't bother coming."

"Then why you here now?" Beth challenged.

"Thought I'd get so good that the coach would have to put me in," I answered.

"And how you going to do that?"

"Practise day and night."

"Can I practise with you?" Beth's eyes pleaded.

"Okay." I relented. Her sad eyes reminded me of Shnitzel and I almost lost it then and there.

"That's great." Beth grinned.

"Only if you don't cramp my style. If you slow me down, you're out."

"Deal." We shook hands on it.

The whistle interrupted us. Coach Wilcox yelled, "You two playing or what?"

"Coming," I shouted. We joined the group.

We did drills for an hour. Two-at-a-time, we took the soccer ball and passed it back and forth to our partners as we ran down the field. In the next exercise, we took shots at the goalie. I missed for the third time.

"Jacobs, do you need glasses?" Coach Wilcox taunted.

My face turned red as I went to the back of the line. I'm defence not forward. I can't score for beans. What does he expect from me? That's not my position. Wait 'till the coach sees me guard our side. Then he'll let me play, I hoped.

The next drill was headers. The coach threw the ball at our heads and we butted it back.

"Your forehead, Beth, not your nose," said the coach. Beth's eyes watered as she rubbed her sore nose. I could tell it really hurt.

The last half hour we divided the team in half. "Bibs against shirts," the coach explained. "Lisa, you play goalie for the bibs."

"I suck at goalie. I play defence," I complained.

"You suck at everything," Coach Wilcox rebutted.

My face turned red and I shut up. I really tried, but two goals got past me.

"It's not fair," Arla complained. "The bibs work hard to score while the shirts get easy goals with Lisa as keeper."

She used to be my friend. Now she's turned against me. I swallowed hard. The game dragged on and on.

The bib team all yelled at me as I let in one goal after another. I felt like the whole world was against me.

19

I<small>T WAS A LONG EVENING</small>. I <small>HAD</small> to go early to the field because Sharon's team had practice before mine. I hated waiting.

Sharon had to wait for me while I had my practice, but she didn't mind because she fooled around in the park with her friends. The difference was she had friends and I didn't.

Later, when Dad picked us up from the practice, Sharon wouldn't shut up. She went on and on about all the points she scored. I wanted to put a gag on her.

"My champ. What about you Lisa? How did it go?" Dad asked, enthusiastically.

"Okay, I guess." I shrugged.

"Make any good saves?"

"Lots," I lied.

"Way to go, Lisa. I'm proud of you."

That made me feel even worse. I tried to figure it out. Why can't the coach just listen to me? I'm wicked at playing defence. Why can't he let me play what I'm good at?

"Lisa's fibbing," Sharon tattled. "Me and my friend stopped to watch. Lisa let in all the shots and her team mates yelled at her, but the other side loved her." She laughed.

"Shut up," I said.

"Cut it out, Lisa." Dad frowned. "Why did you lie?"

I crossed my arms over my chest. "I don't want to talk about it. Okay?"

"No, it's not okay." Dad raised his voice. He spent the rest of the trip home lecturing me about lying. I slouched in my seat while Sharon looked smug.

Nobody understands me. I'm going to run away.

20

THE DUST MADE ME SNEEZE AS I pulled out my overnight bag from the attic. I stuffed in a supply of food. Cookies, chips and two cans of pop. That should do it. Huffing and puffing I shoved my clothes and soccer ball into the bulging bag. A knock at my bedroom door made me jump and I tossed the bag underneath my bed. "Come in."

Mom walked in. "Lisa, I want to talk to you."

"What about?"

"You seem so down." She wrung her hands.

I shrugged.

"I have an idea," said Mom.

"What?" I asked.

"I know your birthday is in July, but since so many of your friends are going away this summer, maybe you'd like to have your birthday party next week, before school gets out."

I hugged my mother. "That's a great idea."

She smiled.

I started talking a mile-a-minute. "I want a soccer party and a sleepover, too. Can you get me a horror movie? Maybe *Blood, Sweat and Gore*? I'll go with you to pick it out."

"That sounds like fun. If you want, I'll bake you a cake? How about I make it in the shape of a soccer ball?"

"You can do that?" I asked.

"Sure. My baking classes weren't for nothing."

"Great. I'll go make invitations on my computer." I looked up and saw Sharon standing at the door. She was shifting from foot to foot.

"Can I help?" she asked sheepishly.

"Why not? You can help me make a list of junk food that we need."

"What about loot bags?" Sharon asked all animated.

"Yeah. We need to buy good stuff," I said.

"We need lots of candy." Sharon got out a piece of paper and started writing down a list.

"You girls seem to have everything under control. I'll go and do some vacuuming." Mom smiled and left the room.

It felt good to be happy again. Thirteen — finally a teen. Who do I want at my party? I nibbled on my pencil as I wrote down names. "I'll invite Beth, Nancy, Janis, Arla, Linda, Samantha, Lily and . . . let me see . . . hey, why not invite everybody on my soccer team too?"

"Sounds great. Can I come?" Sharon asked.

Things were finally back to normal. Sharon was acting like a younger sister again. Just the way it should be. I smiled. "You can come, but you can't stay up for an all-nighter with us. You're too young."

"Please," Sharon whined. "I'll give you my water gun super-shooter for a day."

"Make it a week and you've got yourself a deal," I bargained.

"Deal. Can we have water balloons?"

"All right. Put it on the list. This is going to be some party."

Sharon nodded, enthusiastically.

The rest of the afternoon was spent at the computer, making cards and lists. The cards came out great. Sharon found a graphic with kids playing soccer that was perfect for the front of the card. The inside had all the info, including time and place. I had Sharon add a graphic of teens dancing.

Shopping for loot bags was fun too. Sharon and I picked out fun candy like wax lips, sucker pacifiers, and jawbreakers.

Next, we went to the dollar store and I bought puzzles, funky lipsticks, stickers for nails, and fake tattoos. Sharon and I had a blast.

At home, we divided the stuff and put them in the loot bags. This stuff was really cool. We were going to have so much fun putting on the make-up and tattoos, and eating all of the junk food. We would go to the park to play soccer and come back and have a water fight. Then we would eat some more and stay up all night watching scary movies and talking. I couldn't wait until Monday to give out the invitations.

It wasn't until I went to bed that I remembered about my packed overnight bag stashed underneath the bed.

I'll run away after my party.

21

THE NEXT DAY BETH CAME OVER AND we worked on our passes. "You're hopeless." I shook my head.

Beth looked down at her feet.

"How am I going to get better practising with you? You can't even pass the ball at a standstill. How are you going to kick on the run in a game?"

"I'm sorry, okay?" Beth said.

"Listen, I'm not mister nice guy. I'm only doing this to improve, so I'll get to play in a game."

"You've been playing since you were five and I just started this year. Give me a break." Beth blinked back the tears.

I felt like a heel. "Look, I need a challenge, so if you improve, that will make me work harder. Let's get to it. Kick with the instep not the toe. Like this." I demonstrated. "Now you try."

Beth kicked the ball back to me. "You've got it," I cheered. A big smile spread across Beth's face. "Let's do it again." We passed the ball back and forth. I faked to the right and Beth fell for it and missed. We kicked back and forth, falling into a rhythm.

It started to rain, but we ignored it. "Watch my feet," I instructed. I didn't mind getting soaked; in fact, it was fun. I lifted my leg to kick and fell in the mud. Beth laughed at me so I tackled her. Feeling reckless, we wrestled in the muck. Mom called us in when it started to lightening and thunder.

Of course, Mom had a fit when she saw us. We were covered head-to-toe in mud. She wouldn't even let us into the house until she hosed us down on the lawn. We changed into dry clothes and sat down to have hot chocolate.

We wrote out strategies for a game until my stomach rumbled. I found Mom in the den reading. She had a faraway look as if she was a character in the story. "Mom, Mom." I shook her.

"Huh?"

"Can Beth stay for dinner?"

"Is it that time already?"

"Can she?" I asked, impatiently.

"Only if her mother says yes."

Beth phoned home and got the go-ahead.

I passed Beth another piece of lasagna and we both dug in. Dessert was chocolate pudding. I held my stomach and groaned, "One more bite and I'm going to burst."

Beth took a mouthful. "I've got a joke. A fat guy pigs out and his friend offers him a mint. The fat guy says, 'If I eat one more bite, I'm going to explode,' and his friend says, 'One little mint won't make a difference. Here, eat it.' The fat guy pops the mint into his mouth and explodes like a balloon."

"Gross." We both held our sides laughing. I was impressed that my not-so-thin friend could make a fat joke. I wish I could be that self-confident.

The next morning, as soon as I got to school, I handed out the invitations. Nancy and Janis gave me high fives.

"I'll bring my goalie's gloves," Penny announced.

"I've got some scary stories to tell, when lights are out," Lily announced.

"I'll bring my ghetto blaster," Nancy promised.

"I've got the top-ten songs taped," Janis added.

I felt on top of the world. My party was going to be a hit. This high feeling stayed with me all day long as everybody talked about my party.

Nothing was going to spoil this party.

22

As soon as I arrived at practice, I handed out the invitations.

"What's this?" Tanya asked.

Tanya was the most popular girl on the team. She stuck out her hips and waved the invitation in my face. I gulped. I was already regretting inviting her. "It's for my birthday party."

"Hey, you guys. The wimp is inviting us to her wimpy party," taunted Tanya.

Penny came over. She grabbed one of the cards. "Are you going to have clowns and play duck-duck goose?" Penny teased. The rest of the team gathered round, joining in on the fun.

"Can I have a birthday hat? Is Mommy going to give the birthday girl a kiss?" Tanya snickered. "I'm not going to no sucky party." She tore the card in half and threw it on the ground. Penny copied her.

Coach Wilcox called out. "Enough yackety-yak. In and out of the pylons. Two lines. Move it."

As we lined up, I overheard my team mates making comments. "I'm not going. You going? No way," said another.

Beth stood next to me in line. "Don't mind them. I'll be there," she promised.

I went through the drills, but couldn't concentrate.

Coach Wilcox started picking on me. "Faster, Lisa, faster. You wearing lead shoes?"

The more he yelled, the more I messed up.

"Great teamwork Tanya and Penny," called the coach. Both girls smiled.

When Beth and I were too close together instead of spread out he'd yell, "What do you girls think — that you're married?"

I couldn't concentrate. How did I let my mother talk me into having a birthday party? I was never so humiliated in all my life. Nobody wanted to come.

When practice ended, I made a beeline for the parking lot. Beth caught up. "Don't let them get to you."

I shrugged.

"Don't worry, you still have all your friends from school coming, and I'm going to be there."

I forced a smile.

"We'll have a great time. We don't need Tanya, Penny or any of them."

"You're right. It's going to be great." Mostly, I was trying to convince myself.

23

SHARON HELPED ME FILL THE BALLOONS WITH water. We hung streamers all over the basement. I showed Sharon what went into each loot bag. Mom brought out the cake.

"Wow." My eyes grew big. The cake was half a sphere of butter cake sitting on a chocolate bottom covered with black and white squares of icing. It really looked like a soccer ball coming out of the cake.

With everything ready, and even though it was early, I put on my shin pads and soccer shoes. Then I paced and looked out the window.

The phone rang. "Lisa, it's for you," Dad called.

"Coming." I picked up the phone.

"Hi, it's me, Janis."

"You're late," I said.

"I, ah, can't come. My mother won't let me," Janis whispered.

"Is it about my asthma, again?"

"Yeah."

"But it's my house, so I'm not going to sue," I said. "Let me talk some sense into her."

"Forget it. Believe me, I tried. My mother's really on the warpath. Sorry."

I slammed down the phone. Who needed her anyway? There were enough kids coming without her.

I went back outside to wait.

A car pulled up the driveway. Beth got out carrying a present. I ran over. "You're the first one here. Everybody's ten-minutes late."

"Slowpokes, that's all. Here's your present."

"Thanks."

"Lisa, the phone," Dad called.

This time it was Nancy. "Lisa, I can't come," she blurted out.

I had to sit down. "Why?"

I could hear Nancy whispering to her mother. "What should I tell her? . . . Um, Lisa, my mother says I got to go to my aunt's. Bye."

The click sounded loud in my ear. It was hard to swallow. Beth came over, stuffing chips into her mouth. "Whassup?"

"Now, Nancy can't come."

The phone rang again. "I'm not answering it." I walked back to the window. I called to my mother, "Take a message."

"That was Lily . . . "

"Let me guess," I interrupted. "She can't come."

Mom looked at me with pity in her eyes. I quickly went back outside, slamming the door behind me.

Half an hour went by. Beth and I sat on the porch steps waiting. I could hear the phone ringing inside. I knew that it was for me and that it wasn't good news. My mother stopped calling me. Sharon pulled leaves off the tree and tore them into teeny tiny pieces.

I fought back the tears. *Happy Birthday to me*, I thought bitterly.

24

Beth spoke up. "No point in letting these water balloons go to waste. Let's throw them."

"Yeah," Sharon piped in.

I carried the water balloons in a bag to the front yard. I picked one up and threw it with all my might. It hit the garage and burst. "That feels good." I put everything I had into throwing one after another.

"I'm aiming for the tree," said Sharon. She missed and her water balloon headed for a car stopped at the stop sign. The driver's window was wide open. SPLASH!

Water dripped down his head.

We didn't wait to see his reaction. We ran and hid. Then keeled over laughing.

Later, we pigged out on all the food while we watched two horror flicks.

"Want to hear a scary story?" I asked.

"Sure," said Sharon.

Beth nodded as we huddled close.

I began. "This is the story about Mutilated Samuel." I told the story the way it was told to me in the hospital.

"Sick," said Sharon.

Beth jumped. "Is Mutilated Samuel a real story?"

"I'm just pulling your leg . . . or is it a hand?" I asked.

Beth laughed and Sharon groaned.

We took turns telling scary stories late into the night. "I'll leave the night light on, so you can find the bathroom easier," I said. But I really left it on for me. All of these stories were giving me the heebie-jeebies.

In the morning, I opened up Beth's present. "Spiderman comic books! Great! I don't have these. Let's read them." We did that until lunch. More pigging out. "I can't eat another bite or I'll explode."

"How about a mint?" Beth asked.

We burst out laughing.

"Let's play soccer," I suggested.

"Okay," Beth agreed.

"Let's go." Sharon grabbed her soccer shoes and put them on.

We played for a while, but then we got too hot.

"Water fight!" Beth cried.

"I get your water super-gun, Sharon. That's the deal we made."

"Yeah, yeah." Sharon handed over her gun. She picked up a small squirter. Beth got stuck with a cracked gun that leaked.

"Not fair," Beth cried, as I slaughtered her. Then Sharon and Beth ganged up on me. But it was no contest because my super-gun lasted longer and could shoot further, until Beth ran to the garden hose and aimed it at me full blast.

"Cheater," I cried. Beth got me good so I wrestled with her to grab the hose. Then I went after Sharon. We screamed and laughed, soaking everything in sight. Then we dried off and collapsed on our towels.

"What about the loot bags?" Sharon asked.

"Great idea." I ran through the house.

"My floors!" Mom yelled, as I dripped water everywhere.

"Sorry, Mom." I grabbed the loot bags and ran back out. We opened up all the loot bags and divided the stuff evenly between the three of us.

After Beth left, I unpacked my suitcase. I'm even too pathetic a coward to run away. I got into bed and stared at the ceiling. Now I could let my true feelings out. Only one friend came to my birthday party. I cried silently into my pillow.

25

At school, my friends were too embarrassed to look me in the eye. Great, instead of my party making things right, it made things worse. Again, I ate alone.

At recess, I slouched against the wall. I couldn't wait until school ended. To make matters worse, I had a doozey of an asthma attack. The spray hardly helped at all, so Mrs. Taylor sent me home.

Dad made my tent and I sat under the kitchen table with the kettle going full blast. It felt like a sauna. Slowly, my chest loosened up and I coughed up the phlegm. My wheezing calmed down.

"I'm taking you to Dr. Bellows," my mother insisted.

"I feel better now, honest."

"I already called for an appointment."

"Then cancel it."

"The secretary did me a favour to squeeze you in, so you have to show up. No more arguing. "

"Fine," I relented.

In the waiting room, I wheezed. Another girl also wheezed. "What a chorus," the secretary joked.

Dr. Bellows called me in. She listened to my chest with her stethoscope. It was cold and made me flinch when it touched my bare skin.

"I've heard worse. Nothing to get concerned about," she said directly to my mother. "Give the medication a chance to kick in. Don't worry, it will calm down." She ruffled my hair. "Stay away from dairy products for a few days because they're mucus-forming."

"Should we make another steam tent?" Mom asked.

"The steam tent was just a quick temporary measure. I'm prescribing a Nebulizer. You can use it instead of the tent."

"The Nebulizer sounds like some kind of science fiction machine," I said.

The doctor laughed. "I guess it does sound kind of out of this world, but it's easy to use. It turns liquid medicine into a mist that you inhale through a mask. The bronchodilator medicine relaxes the muscles in the airway walls and helps open the airways." She handed Mom the prescription.

Mom thanked the doctor and we went home.

Twice I cancelled soccer practice with Beth because I didn't feel up to it. On Tuesday, I missed team practice.

Beth showed up at the door after I cancelled our third practice in a row. "What are you doing here?" I asked.

"What's the matter with you?" Beth pushed her way past my arm and made herself comfortable in the den.

"Nothing."

"How come you keep missing practices?" she challenged.

"Don't feel like it, that's all." I shrugged.

"That's no excuse. You're breaking your promise. If you don't practise, how are you going to be good enough to play in a game?"

"Don't care."

"Yes, you do. You're just feeling sorry for yourself. Lisa, what gives?"

"I'm tired. Maybe another day."

"Yeah, right." Beth stormed out.

Mom and Dad looked at me. There was pity in their eyes. They talked to each other in low voices. Next thing I knew, they handed me my birthday present.

"But my real birthday isn't until July."

"You seem a little down," said Dad. "Your mother and I thought that you could use cheering up."

When I tore off the wrapping paper, my eyes nearly popped out of my head. "A camera! It's way too expensive."

Dad's face fell and Mom had pinched lips. "No really, I love it. It's amazing."

Mom smiled.

"You should see the zoom lens this sucker has." Dad immediately started to give me lessons. He showed me how to put the film in and I took shots of flowers and insects in the garden. I giggled as I took close-ups of Dad's nose. For a while, I forgot about my fiasco of a birthday party. Dad made funny faces as I snapped away.

"I've got to go meet with a client. See you later, honey."

"Thanks again, Dad." I photographed him on the way out as he waved goodbye.

Alone, I allowed my feelings to surface. I played with the zoom lens: zoom in, zoom out; fade in, fade out. The soccer birthday party that never happened knocked everything out of me. I just wanted to fade away.

26

"Ten, nine, eight, seven, six, five, four, three, two, one." B-r-r-i-n-g-g, went the school bell. "Yippee!" we screamed, throwing our books into the air. Students pushed by Mrs. Taylor and made a mad dash for freedom.

Everybody talked at once. "I'm going to a sleepover camp," said Janis.

"My family's going to the cottage," said Nancy.

Where was I going? Nowhere. I clutched my report card in my hand. The teacher told us to wait until we got home to open it, but nobody listened. Everyone compared marks. I tore mine open. Straight 'Bs'. *That's me*, I thought, *average and ordinary*. I went over to Nancy. "Want to come over and kick the ball around?"

"Can't. We're leaving right away for the cottage."

"When you coming back?" I asked.

"Be gone all summer," Nancy said.

"Oh." I felt like a balloon with a tiny hole. My happiness was leaking slowly away. "Have a great time."

"You bet." Nancy waved and took off.

"Arla, want to come over?"

"I've got to pack. I'm going away to riding camp. See you in September."

"Bye." Everybody was going away except for me.

At home, I practised kicking the ball against the garage. Sharon's friends went to day camp so she could play with them at night. Mine went to overnight camp and my parents wouldn't let me go away because of my asthma. I wished Shnitzel was here.

I ran inside. "Mom! Can we visit Shnitzel?"

"That's a good idea. I haven't seen my sister in a long time. I'll go phone her."

It was a long ride. I felt car sick, but I couldn't wait to see my dog.

When we arrived, Shnitzel looked at me as if I was some kind of ghost. When he decided I was real, he jumped on top of me licking me to death. "Whoa, Shnitzel, you're smothering me." I finally pushed him off. Then Sharon had her turn at being sat on. We all had a good laugh.

Aunt Irene served us supper. "Shnitzel is very happy with Uncle Ray and me. He has acres of land to run around on. He is busy tending the sheep and herding the strays back into the coral. He has fun barking and bullying the squirrels and raccoons. It's quite a happy life for him."

We finished eating and Mom gathered up the dirty dishes. "Let me help you in the kitchen and we can catch up on old times."

Uncle Ray stood up and patted his belly. "Mighty good dinner, Irene. Why don't I show the kids the horses?"

"Not Lisa. She's allergic to horses."

"Aw, Mom."

"Go visit with Shnitzel."

Shnitzel rested on my lap while I stroked his head. "I'm happy for you, but I'm sad for me. It's lonely without you, boy." I hugged him.

Shnitzel heard the can opener going and he was off in a flash begging for food. I got bored. It's not fair. I wanted to go horse back riding too. But how was I going to get past my mother? And how was I going to convince Uncle Ray?

Mom was busy looking at the family photo album when I walked into the room. "Lisa, come see a picture of you on a pony."

"I'm so small." I have to hurry up and convince her. "Mom?"

"Yes, dear?"

"Can I just go watch everybody saddle up? Please?"

"Fine, but don't get too close or you might get an attack."

I hoped that they hadn't saddled up yet and started on their trail ride. I had to hurry or I'd be too late.

27

I RAN OUT TO THE BARN. "MOM CHANGED her mind, Uncle Ray. She let me come."

"As long as it's fine with your mother." Uncle Ray looked at my father.

He shrugged. "She's the boss."

"But . . . " Now what? I meant Mom let me come and *watch*, not ride. Uncle Ray had misunderstood, but there was no way I was going to correct him.

"Can we go riding? Can we? Can we?" Sharon asked, excitedly.

"Sure thing, kids. Sharon, you can ride Lady." Uncle Ray held the reins of a chestnut horse. "Why don't you brush her down?"

Sharon was in seventh heaven as she brushed Lady.

"You're doing a great job. Remember to use circular motions."

Sharon started brushing Lady's back in little circles.

"That a girl," said Uncle Ray.

Her horse neighed. "I think she likes it," said Sharon.

Uncle Ray laughed as he led out a beautiful black horse with white patches. "Lisa, help me saddle up Stormy," he said.

It took us a while and I kept looking towards the house, worrying that Mom might see me and make me stay. Finally, we got into a single line and headed out to the trail.

Stormy kept stopping in the woods every few feet to eat. I tugged at the reins. "Go Stormy."

"Kick him," yelled Uncle Ray.

"Come on." I kicked, yanked, talked nice, talked mean and I even yelled but nothing worked. "I can't stop him from eating."

"Got to show him who's boss," said Uncle Ray.

"I'm trying."

"Yank harder; talk firm; hold on to those reins so his head can't go down."

I tugged so hard my hands cramped. "Go Stormy," I said, firmly. Away he went — for a few feet, that is — then he stopped for some leaves. This time, I yanked his head away. Sharon had no trouble getting Lady to move.

All of a sudden, Dad's horse bucked. "Whoa," he cried. "Why did he do that?"

"Sh-sh." Uncle Ray pointed to the right.

A deer with its fawn were chewing at the saplings near the edge of the forest.

I watched in amazement at how close we were to the deer. They stood still as statues, then put up their white tails and dove deep into the forest.

Later, when we arrived back and I got off the horse, I walked funny. My legs hurt, but I felt fantastic.

That is, until I saw Mom heading towards me.

28

"... AND YOU WENT BEHIND MY BACK! YOU are grounded. No television for a week." She finished her tirade.

Riding and seeing that deer was worth being grounded.

We went back to the house. Out of nowhere, I started to wheeze. I tried to hold my breath and walk away so Mom wouldn't hear, but it was too late.

"Told you so," she went on.

"I get asthma anyway, so I might as well have fun."

"Some fun — watching my daughter turning blue."

I would have argued more, but I went into a coughing fit. Mom handed me my puffer and waited for it to kick in.

Whimpering, Shnitzel came over to me and sat in my lap licking my face. I could feel my chest tighten, but I wouldn't stop patting him.

We had homemade apple pie and ice cream. Uncle Ray took out his guitar and we sang late into the night. I belted out the songs.

Yawning, Sharon and I were sent to our room. I got the lower bunk bed. I slept in and woke up with Shnitzel licking my face. I was so happy to see Shnitzel, but then my breathing got ragged and I knew that I could never have him back.

Aunt Irene flipped pancakes. At the breakfast table, I stuffed myself with a stack of them loaded with fresh strawberries and real maple syrup. It was so yummy.

"Time to work off that food," said Uncle Ray.

I got to feed the chickens. I discovered that they do have a pecking order. The bossy one always got the food first and the smaller chicken got chased away by the others. I threw some feed to the little chicken that gobbled it up fast.

I wanted to stay longer, but Dad had to meet up with a client, so it was time to go.

Saying goodbye again to Shnitzel was even harder than the first time. He kept trying to get into the car with us, not understanding.

Uncle Ray had to drag him into the house. I could hear his howling as we pulled away. I put my hands over my ears. This was way too hard. I don't know if I can ever visit him again.

29

I WISH WE COULD HAVE STAYED LONGER AT the farm. It didn't matter that I was grounded from television. Oh well, nothing but re-runs on anyway. And all the kids were at camps, cottages or travelling. The street seemed like a ghost town. Sharon talked Mom into sending her to sports camp. I never thought I'd miss her, but there was absolutely nobody to hang out with.

I sifted through the mail. My parents sure got a lot of bills. There were a lot of flyers and advertising. I started to read a pamphlet with kids on the front playing soccer. My hands started to shake. There were openings at a soccer camp not far from my house. I clutched it to my chest. I picked up the phone. "Beth, there are openings at Camp Soccer Fun."

"I'm already signed up," said Beth, "And I can't wait until it starts. Why don't you go too? It will be so much fun."

"I'll ask my mother and call you right back."

Quickly I filled in the form. All I needed was a cheque and a signature, but how was I going to convince my mother?

Mom's forehead furrowed as she keyed in a letter on the computer. To earn pocket money, she typed out legal letters while listening to tapes. "Don't bother me; I've got a deadline to meet."

I remembered the signed autograph of the world's gold medal kayaker Renn Chrichlow. I ran upstairs and found it on my dresser. I re-read it. "To Lisa, Champions Never Give Up."

I showed it to my mother. "Please, can I go to soccer camp?"

"I will pay for your camp, but only if you do extra chores around the house." She made a long list and handed it to me.

I studied the list. I would have to clean the bathrooms, empty the garbage, do the laundry, be nicer to my little sister . . . I cringed.

"Do we have a deal?" asked Mom.

"It's a deal." Yes, I'm going to soccer camp!

Immediately, I called Beth. "I'm in." Beth had to hold the phone away from her ear as I shouted, "Soccer camp here we come!"

The next morning, I stood outside half an hour early, waiting for the camp bus. I checked through my bag for the third time to make sure I had everything. So many yellow school buses with camp names went by and each time my heart beat faster as I strained to read the name. Finally, my bus pulled up. It read, "Camp Soccer Fun." What a sucky name. Did I make a mistake coming here?

The diesel fumes made me dizzy and I sat by myself with the window wide-open trying not to puke. Kids chattered excitedly.

Finally, we screeched to a halt. The brakes on this bus needed oiling. Scanning the field, I searched for Beth. I didn't recognize anyone here. I sighed with relief when I saw Beth. She waved and I ran right over.

Counsellors with clipboards went to the front.

What if we weren't on the same team? I worried.

30

THE CAMP DIRECTOR INTRODUCED THE STAFF.

The little kids were put into teams first. Beth and I held hands praying that we got on the same team.

The camp director announced. "This is one of our senior counsellors. Header, call your team."

"Must be a nickname," I whispered to Beth.

"Lisa Jacobs," Header called. She was short with spiky black hair.

"Here." I jumped up and stood behind her.

Three other names were called. I held my breath. "Beth Willis."

"Yes!" I cried.

The counsellor smiled as Beth ran over and hugged me. We both jumped up and down.

"Just call me Header. After you see me play soccer you'll figure out why."

Most of us laughed.

We followed our counsellor to a tent. "Dump your stuff here because we're meeting at 'the pit.' That's the name of our meeting spot where we sit on the logs in a circle." We ditched our bags and headed for the pit.

"This here is my assistant, Giant." We gasped as we looked up. "I like to head the ball, that's how I got the name Header. Giant's name, well, I think you can guess why she's named that." Giant was all legs and her thighs were the size of tree trunks. She tied her hair back in a ponytail. "I'm on the Varsity team and I love kids who act silly and make funny faces like this." She stuck out her tongue and rolled her eyes. Nervous laughter filled the air.

"I play offence in the Varsity team with Giant," Header explained. "I may be tiny, but anyone is tiny beside Giant." She opened up a bag of balls. "Enough talk; let's do what you guys came here to do. Everybody grab one and follow me to the field."

"Header's cool," I whispered to Beth.

It didn't take long to see that Header was good. I mean really good. Giant and Header passed up and down the field. Header moved like lightning while Giant moved with power.

The counsellors came back, not even out of breath. "Two teams." Giant divided us down the middle. "I want to see what you've got."

Header handed me a red bib. "Pick your position."

"Right defence," I said.

"Go for it." Header gave me a high five.

I played like I'd never played before. The ball couldn't get past me. I dribbled the ball, trying out some of my fancy footwork. My opponent couldn't touch the ball. The whistle blew.

Giant sat us around. "I've been around and I've seen teams. I usually get stuck with the whiners who hate camp and want to play video games all day. The Good Lord must like me because you guys are the best team I've ever had. We'll whomp the whole camp."

We let out a cheer.

"Let's break for lunch." Everybody got up. Giant stopped me. "Lisa, you are dynamite. Without a good defence, we're sunk and you are the best. Where have you been hiding?"

I beamed.

"You on a team?"

"In the evenings, but the coach never lets me play?"

Giant looked shocked. "Why?"

"Because I have . . . " I cleared my throat. If I told her would she decide not to let me play too?

"Spit it out, Lisa."

"Asthma," I said under my breath.

Giant's face clouded over.

Now I've done it. Why couldn't I keep my big mouth shut?

"What a jerk not to play the top player. I've never seen anyone cover like you do. You're so focussed. You're the best and I mean it."

I walked away feeling on top of the world.

But the two teams were worlds apart. With Appliance Reliance I was a nobody and here I could do no wrong. But I was still the same person, Lisa. Go figure.

Now that the camp day was done, the loser was back.

31

No sooner had I gotten off the bus when Mom came out of the house heading straight for the car. "Hurry up; you've got a check up with Dr. Bellows."

I groaned. "But I'm hot and thirsty."

Mother smiled. "That's why I brought you a drink in the car. And, I'll put on the air conditioning. Move it."

Mom dropped me off in front of the medical building. "I've errands to run so I'll come up when I'm done."

"But . . . " The car took off before I could finish my sentence.

I took the elevator and went into the waiting room. It was crowded so I knew that I was in for a long wait. Thumbing through the magazines, I selected one on sports. I flipped through the pages until I saw an article about a Canadian Mount Everest team whose athletes had asthma. I read on. "They've reached the summit. Not only is mountain climbing dangerous and strenuous, but the higher you climb, the colder it gets and the air thins and they can do this with asthma."

"Lisa, Lisa, it's your turn," repeated the secretary. Blushing, I followed her in.

Dr. Bellows examined me. "I give you a good bill of health. What have you been doing differently?"

"I'm in soccer camp."

"All this fresh air and exercise seems to be working miracles. You've got a strong set of lungs. Keep up the good work."

And to think that my first doctor wanted to keep me in isolation, hiding away and having no life. He was from the old school where I couldn't do any exercise. I gave Dr. Bellows a kiss on the cheek.

"What was that for?" she asked smiling.

"For being such a wonderful doctor," I said.

Mom was waiting for me. When I left the office, I couldn't stop thinking about the story of the Canadian mountain climbers. I can't believe they have asthma like me. If they can climb a mountain, then for sure I can be a strong soccer player.

Everyday after camp, between evening soccer practices, I was glued to the television, watching the Olympics. It was so exciting to see the best in the world compete. I watched an interview with Silken Laumann. The announcer says, "I am with Silken Laumann who is walking to her event with a cane and a brace. Do you have anything to say to your fans?"

Silken says to the camera, "Work hard, and be the best that you can be."

I took her words to heart and imagined myself playing in the next game.

But that happy feeling soon wore off as I saw Beth once again sitting on the sidelines and I realized that Coach Wilcox would stop me, yet again, from playing.

I dragged myself over to Beth and sat down. "I don't know why I keep coming. Coach Wilcox hasn't let either of us play in a game. I'm getting tired of cheering the team on. I don't even feel part of the team."

"Don't give up, Lisa. One day he'll have to use us."

"Be realistic, Coach Wilcox isn't going to take a chance with us." I pulled up blades of grass. "Our team is struggling to qualify for the playoffs and every game counts. There is no way the coach will let us play."

Beth looked as miserable as me. Now I felt guilty. The truth hurt and I was really hurting, but why did I have to bring Beth down too? Her head hung and her hair covered her face. I think she was crying. I had to say something to cheer her up. "Beth, I'm sorry. Maybe I'm dead wrong."

"What are you talking about?" asked Beth.

"Well, it was . . . it was my horoscope! Today it said, 'The stars are with you and you will get your wish'."

"Really?" Beth looked hopeful.

"Really." The knot in my stomach went away. I hadn't really read my horoscope, but it always says *something* like that. I picked up a dead dandelion and blew the little seed parachutes and watched them fly away. If the seeds stayed in the air while you watched, then your wish was supposed to come true. I watched as the seeds blew out of sight. I wished that Coach Wilcox would put Beth and me into the game.

32

Beth and I cheered the team on. They really needed it because they were being slaughtered. We shouted and jumped up and down.

"Lean to the left, lean to the right, stand up, sit down, fight, fight, fight!" we yelled.

There was a stop in play when Lily and Samantha left the field.

"Get back in there, girls," cried Coach Wilcox.

"We need a break," gasped Lily.

"The other team is running us into the ground," panted Samantha. She held onto the cramp in her side. "Let the subs take over."

"You girls are the best defence we have. Hang in there a little longer. You can do it."

No sooner did the two tired defence players go back in when Samantha headed the ball with her face instead of her forehead, and her nose started to bleed. When Lily stopped to help her friend, a defender on the other team immediately tripped her. Both girls had to be helped to the sidelines. The referee blew his whistle and Coach Wilcox was forced to call in substitutions. Since all his other players were on, he pointed at Beth and me. "You're both in," he grumbled.

Maybe the stars were on my side, although I felt bad that Samantha and Lily had hurt themselves. This as not the way I dreamed of getting into the game, but this was my big chance.

Beth and I immediately jumped up and ran onto the field. We put into action everything we'd learned at soccer camp. We both had each other's moves down pat from practising so much together and we got ready to pass and receive. It was obvious that the other team was far better, but I could see that they were short of players and had no subs. They were playing tired while Beth and I were fresh and full of life. Because of our high bursts of running and blocking, things started to turn around for our team who fed off us.

Beth and I passed back and forth to each other, out-running and out-manoeuvring our opponents. Our forwards took over and scored.

When it was over, Lily patted me and Beth on the backs. "You helped tie the game for us." The rest of the team came over to congratulate us.

"Coach, where have you been hiding this talent?" asked Rachel.

Coach Wilcox looked at me and Beth, amazed. "What do you know? You girls have really improved. Those drills at practice paid off, right?"

"Right, Coach." I winked at Beth. I'm sure the drills helped, but we knew we learned most of our soccer skills from playing everyday at soccer camp. Not only were the lessons better, but so was the camp's positive approach to play, making it fun and inspiring. Coach Wilcox played to win. That was obvious when he wouldn't use us as subs. But I now hoped that things had changed because Beth and I had proven ourselves.

The next day at camp, Header taught us how to head the ball with our foreheads. We got into partners and took turns throwing the ball high while the other one headed it back. Then we played an older group and were killed.

Giant took us swimming afterwards. She looked great in a bikini. I hoped one day that I would get curves.

"You guys were great!" said Giant.

"What are you talking about? We lost!" I waded into the pool.

"Yeah, but you played the biggest, toughest team and held your own. Sure, we could have played an easier team and won. But I'd rather you learn to lose and realize that it's not everything and life goes on. Want to play them again?"

"Yeah!" I cried with the others.

The cold water of the swimming pool felt refreshing. I floated on my back seeing pictures in the clouds. It was hard to believe, but I actually felt good about losing.

33

THINGS COULDN'T BE BETTER BECAUSE I WAS living and breathing soccer. We played all day at soccer camp and in the evening, Coach Wilcox was using us as subs more.

I was feeling tired, but a happy tired. Today was Visitors' Day. My father couldn't make it, but my mom was there.

We played hard, but so did the other team. The purple team were the oldest group at camp and most of them had been to this camp the year before.

Header took us aside. "Unfortunately, I had most of these girls in my team last year and they know all of my moves and strategies. Just try to keep the ball in their field because their offense is dynamite."

Beth and I passed to one another, but like Header said, their offence ran circles around us. One father was yelling his head off at number 11, the best offense player. Even though she was awesome, he was screaming at her to do better.

At halftime, I joined my mother as she handed out orange slices to our team. Mom looked really happy as we all ate and joked around.

The whistle blew and we were back on. I ran and covered my opponent. But it was tough because she was zigzagging like a rabbit.

I was huffing and puffing by the time the game ended. We were slaughtered.

But good old Mom handed out homemade butter tarts and my team let out a whoop of joy and dug in.

Meanwhile, the winning team looked sad because none of the parents brought refreshments. That father was still yelling at the star player and she looked miserable even though she won.

I guess winning isn't everything, I thought as I stuffed another tart into my mouth.

My mom was getting compliments for her baking, and some of the mothers were asking for the recipe. She was glowing from all of the attention. I was happy for her. Sharon had my camera and was taking pictures of me and the team. My team. We hammed it up a lot.

We had lost, but I felt like a winner.

34

I WAS EXHAUSTED FROM PLAYING THE GAME ON Visitors' Day, but couldn't let my Appliance Reliance team down by not showing up for practice. So, while Dad drove me to the soccer field, he lit another cigarette. The smoke made me hack and cough even though the window was wide open.

I lost it.

"Dad, if you loved me you wouldn't do that."

My words must have struck a sore spot because my father turned white. He butted out. "That's my last one. I swear."

"That's what you said last time."

"I mean it this time and I'll prove it to you." He parked the car, found a garbage can and threw out his pack of cigarettes.

"Thanks, Dad."

"No problem." He ruffled my hair. I hate that, but he was making an effort to quit cold turkey so I just smiled at him. "Have fun, Lisa."

"I will, Dad." I waited until his car left before I took my spray. I didn't want to upset him that he'd given me asthma with his smoking because he was trying. I joined the team on the soccer field.

We did a lot of drills of running in and out of the pylons. My feet felt like lead, but I still had fun, especially when I got to practise some new moves with Beth. We worked so well together. It was like we knew exactly what the other was thinking.

Finally, we finished the practice then gathered around to chat and snack.

It was Tina's turn to bring our refreshments. As usual, I remembered to ask, "Do the chocolate chip cookies have nuts?"

"No, you can eat them," said Tina.

They were home-baked, with big chunks of chocolate — my favourite. There were enough for seconds and I helped myself. It sure tasted yummy. As I licked my fingers, my throat started to hurt and my tongue started to swell. "I feel funny," I said.

"What's so funny?" asked Beth.

I put my hands on my throat and started to cough.

"You're not joking." Beth ran to her mother. "Call 911, Lisa's throat is closing!"

Her mother pulled out her cell phone and called. By then I was leaning against a tree hacking and wheezing.

Tina came running over. "Omygod. When you started choking, I ran and asked my mother. She says she forgot that she had put in almond extract. I'm so sorry."

I was feeling dizzy and I slid down the trunk of the tree to my knees. It was so hard to breath. My mouth opened and closed like a fish. "My EpiPen," I squeaked.

There was a crowd standing around me.

"Where?" asked Beth.

"In my . . . *wheeze* . . . green knapsack . . . *wheeze* . . . by our team bench."

Beth ran away.

Then everything got hazy.

35

I VAGUELY REMEMBER VOICES FAR AWAY AND THE sound of a siren, a sharp pain in my thigh and a mask being put over my face.

My grandmother always said, "Wear clean underwear just in case you are rushed to the hospital."

"Yes," I said out loud, "I'm wearing my polka-dot, clean underwear." But it came out muffled because of the mask.

When I woke up, I was in a hospital bed. Dr. Bellows stood over me.

"Lisa, you've had an anaphylactic attack where your throat swelled and your air passage was blocked off and air couldn't get in. Fortunately, you had your EpiPen with you and were given adrenalin right away. It takes only 4-6 minutes before it's too late. I'm not saying this to scare you, but to remind you to have your EpiPen with you — always. In an allergic reaction, mouth-to-mouth doesn't work."

I tried to sit up, but had to lie right back down because my head was swimming.

Dr. Bellows read my chart. "You were lucky that your friend reacted quickly. Sometimes, people panic and freeze. Your friend did a fine job of finding your EpiPen. She even jabbed it into your thigh correctly. You need to teach your friends the three 'A' s of anaphylaxis: 'Awareness, Avoidance and Action'."

I looked down at the black and blue mark on my thigh just as Beth and her mother entered the room.

"Sorry about the bruise," said Beth.

"I'll live with it . . . Get it?" Nobody laughed at my sick joke.

Everybody was talking in a forced cheerful voice.

"When will I be allowed out of here?"

"By tomorrow," said Dr. Bellows.

"Can I talk to Beth alone?" I asked.

"Sure," said Dr. Bellows."

Everyone went out to the hall.

"Thanks, Beth," I said.

"It's no biggie."

"Yes. It was a biggie. Just don't let things change between us, okay?" I asked.

"What do you mean?"

"Please don't let your mother freak out and be afraid for you to hang out with me?"

"My mother's cool. She would never do that," said Beth.

"Promise things won't get weird between us?" I asked.

"I promise," said Beth.

The nurse poked her head into the room. "Say goodbye to your visitors; I have to take your blood pressure."

Everyone came back in to say goodbye. "Hey, I'll be out of here in time for the big final game," I told them.

"You're not thinking straight," scolded my mother. "You won't be playing in any soccer game anytime soon."

My face felt hot and flushed. "What are you talking about? Didn't you hear the doctor say that I'll be fine? These are the soccer finals!"

"You're not playing and that's final." Mom crossed her arms.

Before I could say anything else, the nurse shooed everyone out and wrapped a band around my arm and pumped a bulb. "My my, your blood pressure seems unusually high."

I felt so angry that I bet my blood was near boiling point.

"Maybe I should get the doctor."

"I'm just upset. You don't have to get the doctor," I said.

"I'll test it again in an hour." The nurse left.

My energy drained away. I felt like giving up, but a little voice kept saying, Silken Laumann never gives up. Renn Chrichlow never gives up. Champions never give up. I had to find a way to play. But how?

36

I came home from the hospital and my mother started treating me like a delicate flower. I wasn't allowed to do anything or go anywhere. She wouldn't let me out of her sight. She even stopped me when I started to do the chores to pay her back for sending me to camp.

"But how can I pay you back if I can't dust and sweep the floors?"

"Um . . . " I could tell that I stumped her. "You can sit down and tape the recipes that I collect from the newspaper into my cooking binder."

"You sure that won't be too strenuous for me? How many calories do cutting and taping burn?"

"No need to be sarcastic," said Mom. "Would you like another piece of watermelon?"

"My stomach is going to look like I swallowed a watermelon if I don't get up and do some exercise. Come on, Mom, give me some slack?"

"This is as hard on me as it is on you," said Mom.

"Yeah, right," I muttered under my breath. Sharon came into the room and grabbed a piece of watermelon.

"Put that back, young lady. That's for dessert. You'll ruin your appetite," said Mom.

"Then how come Lisa is allowed?"

"Because I said so," said Mom.

I always hated when my mother answered that way. I liked to hear a good reason — not a power-trip answer.

Sharon waited until my mother's back was turned and grabbed a piece of watermelon and popped it into her mouth. Then she smiled at me with her mouth full. It was kind of gross.

I decided to work on my father, so I went to find him. He was in his workshop nailing something into a board. I had no idea what he was making. It didn't matter, because nothing that Dad made seemed to have any function. I think that he just did it to burn off steam.

"Hi, Dad."

"How you doing, Lisa?"

"Dad, I can't take it. It's like I'm in jail. I keep telling Mom I'm fine but she won't listen to me. You've got to do something."

Dad scratched his head. "Give it time. You gave your mother and me a big scare. Humour her for a few days and then she'll loosen up."

"A few days?" I cried. "I don't have a few days. The playoffs start tomorrow."

Dad's eyebrows came together as he frowned. "You're asking too much of us, Lisa. We have your best interests at heart. You were a very sick girl." His throat caught. "We almost lost you."

"Oh, Dad." I hugged him. "It was the nuts that made me sick, not playing soccer."

"I don't care. You were just in the hospital. I need to do the responsible thing . . . "

"But . . . "

"No buts, young lady. You are not well enough. You need to get your strength back. No game and that's final."

The only thing final were the soccer finals and I was going to be there no matter what.

I called Beth up. "I need a plan to get to the soccer finals. Any ideas?"

As I listened to Beth's plans, I got more and more excited. "It's risky, but I'm going for it."

"What are you going for?" asked Sharon as she stood in the hallway.

"Ah, I'm going out for a chocolate bar."

"Mom won't let you go out," said Sharon.

"Then will you buy me one?" I asked.

"We have a couple in the cupboard. Get one yourself," said Sharon.

"Do we? Okay. Do you want one?" I asked.

"No, I'm okay."

Sharon must have had her radar on because she stuck to me like glue. I couldn't get rid of her. What was I going to do? She was going to ruin everything.

37

THE WORST PART WAS MY SISTER WAS being so nice. The only way to ditch her was to get into a fight with her. "Get out of my face," I yelled.

To my surprise, Sharon started to cry. "I know that you're trying to sneak out. I only want to help," she sniffed.

I pulled her by the sleeve. "Shut up. Mom will hear you. Come to the basement and we'll talk." We hurried down the steps.

"I have to play, but Mom and Dad are scared that I am too sick to be in the finals," I explained. "I feel fine."

"What are you going to do?" asked Sharon.

"I was going to sneak out and play in the finals, but I can't hurt Mom and Dad like that. I've got a new plan."

"What?" asked Sharon.

I'll call Dr. Bellows and see if it's all right with her. If she agrees, then I'm sure that Mom and Dad will change their minds."

I called, but the secretary said that the doctor was with a patient. I left a message for the secretary to please ask Dr. Bellows if I was well enough to play and to get back to me A.S.A.P. I hung up.

Time was running out. I paced. Finally, I couldn't stand it any longer. "Sharon, tell Mom and Dad that I've gone to the game, just to watch. I need you to answer the phone and meet me at the soccer field as soon as the doctor's office phones back."

"Okay," said Sharon.

Everything depended on that phone call.

I looked at my watch. The game had already started. I threw on my team jersey and ran out the door. I wanted to play so bad. But could I just sit there and watch from the sidelines?

38

THE GAME WAS A GOOD SIX BLOCKS away and I was so late. There was no bus and I couldn't afford to wait, so I ran the whole way.

By the time I got to the playing field, I was out of breath and wheezing hard. I started to panic. If Coach Wilcox heard me sounding like that, he'd never let me play even if my doctor gave me the go-ahead. I will have ruined everything.

With shaking fingers, I took my puffer from my pocket and put it to my lips and squeezed. It was hard to hold my breath when I was so short of it, but I forced myself. I was supposed to wait another minute before taking another puff. It seemed like an eternity. I inhaled deeply and slowed my breathing. My whistling stopped. I hurried to my team. Beth sat on the sidelines. She greeted me with a hug.

"What's the score?" I asked.

"They're ahead one nothing."

"That sucks," I said.

"We're in big trouble." Beth bit her nails.

"You're late," snapped Coach Wilcox.

"I'm sorry but . . . "

The coach walked away, too caught up in the game. He was busy pacing, waving his hands and shouting at the players, and arguing with the referee about bad calls. Our team just couldn't get control of the ball. The blue team — The Exterminators — was out-running, out-manoeuvring, out-kicking our team. They were running circles around us.

At halftime, our team hobbled off the field. We looked like we had been in a war. Beth's mother served us oranges. This perked us up a little.

"Okay, Beth and Lisa, you're in," said Coach Wilcox.

I was itching to play and I was feeling fine but hadn't gotten permission from my doctor or my parents. Beth ran onto the field. Now was my big chance. What should I do?

"Come on, Lisa," shouted Beth.

I stood there frozen. What would Silken Laumann do? She never quit. I took a deep breath and ran onto the field.

Then I saw my parents heading towards the field. Mom looked like she was ready to do battle. It was over before it even started.

39

"Lisa Jacobs, you get off that field right now!" shouted my mother.

"What's going on?" asked the Coach.

"Lisa was just in the hospital and shouldn't be playing," said my mother. "Tell him, Bill."

My father cleared his throat. "That's right."

Sharon shrugged and gave me an I'm-sorry look with her eyes.

Coach Wilcox stood with his legs apart with his feet firmly planted in the ground. "The team needs her. We're in big trouble right now, and she's our only hope of winning. But if you think that Lisa is too sick too play, then that's that."

The game was back in play and there I was sitting on the sidelines. At that moment, I hated my mother. I couldn't even look at her or my father. Sharon sat beside me, "Sorry, the doctor's office didn't call back."

I shrugged. "Thanks anyway."

Beth went in and paired with Lily. She was holding her own, but Beth didn't have me to pass to her. We had worked out great passing moves. Lily was exhausted and barely covered her position on defence; she never passed to Beth. Tanya, our best forward, was constantly checked by their best player and couldn't keep the ball. It was like watching the Titanic sink and there was nothing I could do about it.

Coach Wilcox didn't help matters. He was yelling at everyone on our team. Our team spirit sank to an all-time low.

Big surprise, our team lost. Coach Wilcox gathered us around. "You guys stank the place out. We lost our chance to get Gold or Silver, but we can still win the Bronze. Go get some oranges and water. Our next game starts in fifteen minutes."

My team mates got in a huddle and started whispering. The next thing I knew, they were coming towards me.

They gathered around me and my parents. Tanya spoke first. "We need Lisa. Please let her play?"

"I'm sorry to disappoint you, girls, but Lisa's health comes first. She can't play," said my mother.

I stood up. "Mom, you trust me right?"

"Of course I do," she said.

"Then trust me to know my own body. Right now, I feel fine. If I start to feel sick then I promise that I will stop playing. Okay?"

The referee's whistle blew. "Appliance Reliance! Get on the field!" he shouted.

I waited for my mother's answer.

There were tears in her eyes. "Hurry up, Lisa. Your team is waiting."

"Dad?"

"Get on the field," he said.

I ran into position. The girls on my team cheered. Beth patted me on the back. Coach Wilcox looked relieved.

Our yellow team took our places on the field. The red team marched in. They looked tall and strong.

The referee announced, "The game is forty minutes. Each half is twenty minutes. There will be a two-minute break between quarters and a four-minute break between halves. Let the game begin."

I was fresh and put a new energy into the team. We started strong, getting to the ball first and keeping it. Ingrid, a tall Swedish girl on our team took the ball and faked a pass to Tanya, but instead passed to me because I was wide open. I dribbled the ball to mid-field. Penny saw the play and raced downfield with a defender close behind. I quickly passed to her. She made a beeline for the net, kicked hard and "Yes!" I cried, as the ball went in.

"We're tied," puffed Beth.

My opponent tried to psyche me out. "Hey kettle! You should be making tea — you're whistling."

"Ha-ha," I said, intercepting the ball and passing it to Tanya. She took it all the way and scored.

We ran and huddled and jumped all over each other. I felt higher than a kite.

But our happiness was short lived as they stole the ball and kicked it high into the corner, making it two-all.

I groaned.

This fired up the red team and they kept control of the ball. Then they scored. Again.

Now they were ahead 3–2. I didn't work so hard just to lose. There were only fifteen seconds to go. I gave Beth the hand signal for play number 6. She nodded and stopped covering her man and so did I. We had nothing to lose as we both moved up the field after the ball. With three of our men on the red striker, I was able to steal the ball. Beth immediately raced towards the side of the net. I took aim and kicked it high to Beth, who headed it in. "Scored!" I cried. I couldn't believe it. Our play worked! Header would be so proud of Beth. The whistle blew. Time's up. My team was all over Beth. They jumped on her and patted her back.

The Coach called us into a huddle. "We're into overtime. The rules say that in a tie game there will be two ten-minute overtime periods. The teams will switch sides at the end of the first overtime period. Let's go and do it!"

We stood in a circle with our fists in the middle and cried, "Fight, fight, with all our might, go yellow!" And we were back in the game.

The clock was ticking and we were pumped, but so was the other team. The red team immediately got hold of the ball and ran with it. The kick to our net was low and powerful. My heart was in my throat. I cheered as our goalie dove to steer the ball wide.

I was keeping close to their best striker and when I saw a chance, I took control of the ball. Beth ran ahead and I passed to her. Her opponent was on top of her, so she kicked it back to me. I faked a pass to her, but instead, I dribbled straight for the net. None of my team mates were there to pass it to, so it was all up to me. I aimed my kick for the right corner of the net, but shanked it into the side of a red player. The ball rebounded into the net. What a fluke. Their goalie looked stunned. My team jumped up and down, screaming.

We were back in play and the red players were as mad as hornets. Number 15 kept harassing Beth, calling her names and pushing her whenever the ref wasn't looking. The red striker was moving towards our goal. Beth moved quickly and cleanly tackled the ball. The red player faked contact and fell. The referee only saw the fall and awarded the red team a penalty kick.

I started to argue, but my coach motioned for me to be quiet, so I shut up. The red team lined up and the kick went in. The whistle blew. The referee signalled for the teams to switch ends. There was no time to be angry. I had to focus.

I was all over my player. I passed to Beth, but her opponent tackled her hard. Beth writhed on the ground holding her ankle. The referee called the foul and stopped the play. I quickly helped Beth to the sidelines.

"I'll take it from here," said the coach as he helped Beth into a chair. Beth's mother ran over with an ice pack. "Lisa, get back on the field. We need you," cried the coach.

Beth gave me the thumbs up and I knew that she would be okay. Both teams played hard, but nobody could score on either side.

The ref blew the whistle and called us all over. "Because the game is still tied at the end of the second overtime period, penalty kicks will be used to break the tie. Here is how it is going to work. Each team selects five players to kick. The players must have been on the field when the second overtime period ended. The teams will alternate kicks. If the game is still tied after the first round of penalty kicks, the game will go into sudden-death penalty kicks," he explained.

Just don't let me be in the sudden-death penalty kick. Please don't pick me, I prayed.

40

Our team lined up. The first girl on our team got ready to kick. "Go Appliance Reliance," we cheered. "Ouch," I groaned, as the ball went to the right of the net.

The red team went. They scored. I bit my fingernails down to the skin. We were down by one.

Our next yellow player lined up. The ball sailed high to the left corner, and whew, it went in. *All right, we could win this*, I thought.

Then red went. "Yes!" I cried as our goalie easily caught the ball. We were still tied.

I heard the sound of a lawn mower and looked over to the field beside us. Just my bad luck; the smell of cut grass triggered my asthma and I started to wheeze.

It was yellow's turn and I crossed my fingers. "Yikes!" I cried as their goalie jumped and stopped the ball from going in.

Red kicked again. I was so glad when Number 15 missed. We were still tied.

Yellow went. I held my breath. "Oh no," I groaned as their goalie stretched out and deflected the ball just wide of the left post.

My asthma was getting worse.

Then the next red went and kicked hard and low. Our goalie made a dive. "Oh, what a great save! We're still tied."

I took out my puffer and sprayed it into my mouth. I held my breath the way I was supposed to so that the medicine would get absorbed.

The last yellow . . . "Come on yellow team!" I yelled. The goalie anticipated the kick and leaned to the right. Tanya faked right, but kicked left and it crossed the goal line. "Yes!" I yelled.

I started coughing.

The last kick for the red team . . . I held my breath. Number 5 kicked the ball at an angle. As our goalie tried to stop the ball, it deflected off of her glove right into the net. My shoulders slumped. The teams were tied again.

My chest was still tight. I had no choice but to take my spray again.

The referee announced. "Both teams are tied. The next step is that each team will alternate and the first team to score, wins."

I couldn't get it out of my head. Whoever gets the next point, wins. The red team went . . . will she get it in? Whew, the ball went wide.

I went over to my mother. "Mom, I am having an attack. What should I do?"

"Did you take your spray?" asked Mom.

I nodded, yes.

"Wait for the medicine to kick in and do your breathing exercises."

I sat there breathing in slow and deep just like the doctor had taught me. Thankfully, it was working because it was getting easier to breathe. "Mom, do you want me to stop playing?"

"You sound a lot better, Lisa. I think that you should be just fine."

My mother's answer surprised me. She was really trying to give me a normal life. "Thanks, Mom." I went back and joined my team.

The coach pointed to Lucy. "It's all up to you."

But the referee shook his head. "She was not on the field when the second overtime period ended. You have to pick someone else who was on the field and has not had a turn kicking yet."

Everyone on my team was staring at me. I felt the blood rush from my head. "But I suck at scoring."

"It's all up to you, Lisa," said Coach Wilcox.

Shaking, I lined up. Why me? This can't be happening. My head was throbbing. The tension was so thick. The red team was heckling me. "Tea kettle! Tea kettle!" they chanted.

They are just trying to psyche me out, I thought. *I have to focus.*

My team looked at me with great expectation. "You can do it, Lisa," someone called. I didn't turn to look. I have to concentrate, I told myself. I pulled back my right foot. It was shaking. This is it. I aimed low. The ball was heading straight for the right corner of the net. *Go in, go in*, I prayed. The goalie dove and deflected it with her hands.

I felt like someone had punched me in the stomach.

It would be okay. The red team would miss and then we would have another chance. Losing the game wouldn't be all my fault.

It was the red team's turn. The tall girl lined up and kicked hard to the left corner. I held my breath as our goalie dove, but couldn't stop the ball from going in.

The red team went wild. My team stood there frozen. We lost the Bronze medal.

Nobody had to say a word. I could see the disappointment in their eyes.

Why hadn't I listened to my parents and not played? At the time, I thought not playing was the worse thing in the world, but now I knew better. Playing and letting your team down was the worse possible thing that could happen. I wished that I was invisible. I walked through the crowd feeling naked. Nothing could have been more humiliating. Sure, it wasn't just me who didn't score, but I wished that I could have saved the day, like a super hero. Just call me super loser.

"Hey, Lisa, good game," called Tanya.

"You were great on defence," said Penny.

Huh? "Ah, thanks," I muttered. I stood there stunned. Maybe I was being too hard on myself. Renn Chrichlow and Silken Laumann would never give up on themselves.

My parents and Sharon were waiting for me. I hugged my mother. "You really helped me." Mom had tears in her eyes. "Dad? Can I invite the team out for pizza?"

"Good idea," he said.

"Sharon, you can bring a friend if you want."

"Thanks." She went off to get her best friend.

I ran after Tanya and Penny. "Wait up," I called. "Do you want to go out for pizza?"

"Sure," said Tanya. "Let's have a team party to celebrate our season together."

"Let me round up the rest of the girls," said Penny.

"I'll help," I said, smiling.

41

I COULDN'T BELIEVE THAT THE SUMMER WAS OVER so fast. Nancy, Janis, Linda and Arla were back from vacation. The first day of school was always exciting. We were now the oldest in the school, the big shots. The little kids looked so lost and small. They looked up to us and some of them were even scared of us.

I used to love the smell of new books and getting new clothes for the first day back. It was always exciting to catch up with all the gossip and see everybody. It was like that for a full five minutes: then all the bad stuff came flooding back.

Nancy and Janis were tight. They had each other and didn't need me. My other friends were indifferent, like I wasn't worth talking to. During soccer camp, I had forgotten about all this.

I have to admit, my summer had its ups and downs. Downs, when Coach Wilcox wouldn't let me play, and highs when I played soccer at camp and got to hang out with Beth. But summer camp was over and the memories were becoming distant. I would miss seeing Beth everyday. She went to a private school where she'd make new friends and be busy with homework and other activities. Would she become a distant memory too?

I wandered around the school yard alone. Since school began, I was beginning to feel like I had leprosy. I had too much time to think. It was going to be a long year.

After supper, I worked on my homework. We had to do a three-minute speech tomorrow in front of the class on any topic. Suddenly, I had a brain flash.

∾ ∾ ∾

The next day, I stood in front of the class. "My topic today is on asthma. I have asthma and sometimes I have trouble breathing. But I am the same person that I was before I got asthma. Yes, sometimes I wheeze, and sometimes I have to sit out and relax until my breathing returns to normal. And sometimes I have to take my medication. Some great Canadians have climbed mountains, won World and Olympic medals, with disabilities. Nothing stopped them. They are my inspiration. Nothing is going to stop me from doing the things that I want to do. Now, I will pass around my puffer for you to look at. Any questions?"

Lots of hands went up. Many of my old friends and soccer team mates had questions about asthma. They seemed really interested. What do you know?

"Want to hang out together after school?" asked Janis.

"What about your Mom?" I asked.

"I'll have to convince her," she said.

"I can give you some literature on asthma, if that would help," I said.

"That's a great idea," said Janis.

"Can I come too?" asked Nancy.

"Only if you bring your soccer ball," said Janis.

42

I CALLED UP BETH AND WE ARRANGED TO meet at the soccer field at her private school. I felt out of place as I saw all of these kids in uniform wearing green plaid skirts and ties. The girls who wanted to be rebellious hiked up their skirts, and guys untucked their shirts and opened a couple of buttons.

Beth saw me and waved. I waved back and ran over. She hugged me. It was so nice to see her.

"I arranged to meet with Giant at Corner Donuts."

"Really?" I asked.

"Yeah, come on. We're late."

We chitchatted on the way to the doughnut shop. "There's Giant sitting by the window." I pointed.

Giant gave us both a high five. "Pick out a doughnut and drink: it's my treat."

"I can't have a doughnut," I said.

"Why not?" asked Giant.

"Nut allergy, but I'll have a tea."

We got our orders and sat down. "Do you wear a special bracelet?" asked Giant.

I showed them my medical-alert bracelet. "I always wear it on my left wrist and I never go anywhere without EpiPens in my fanny pack. Thanks, Giant, for making this summer great," I said.

"We had so much fun," said Beth.

"That's what it's all about. Fun. Just try your best and be the fittest you can be," said Giant.

"I'm so full," said Beth.

"How about a mint," I said.

"I can't or I'll explode." Beth laughed so hard her drink went up her nose and she started snorting. That got Giant and me laughing. I was sure that we would get thrown out but people just smiled back at us.

"Are you two on a soccer team?" asked Giant.

We both shook our heads, no.

"I heard that there are openings on the Rep soccer team. You girls should try out."

"That would be so cool if we both made it on the Rep team," said Beth. "Then we could see each other every week."

"And we could work out some more plays together. We would be unstoppable as defence," I said.

"Let's practise together so that we're in top shape for the tryouts," said Beth.

"Sounds good," I said.

Giant got up. "Good luck in the tryouts. I got to get going. I'm in the university soccer team and I have practice. Can I give you girls a lift home?"

"No, it's okay," I said. "Beth and I will jog to my place. We want to stay fit."

"That's the spirit," said Giant.

"See ya." Giant waved and got into her mini-car. It was the size of a golf cart. Beth and I looked at one another thinking the same thing. How could Giant fit into such a small car? That got as snorting and laughing all over again.

I felt alive and ready to conquer the world. I made up my mind. I was never going to let myself become invisible again. Yes, I have asthma, but it doesn't change who I am. Silken Laumann showed guts and will power in spite of a major injury. She had said, "Work hard, and be the best that you can be." I want to be just like her. After all, champions never give up.

Beth and I started jogging. I shouted, "Tryouts, here I come!"

DEBBIE SPRING has been writing for over twenty years. Her publication, *The Righteous Smuggler*, from The Holocaust Remembrance Series (Second Story Press), was shortlisted for CBC's Young Canada Reads. Her short story "The Kayak" was published in the anthology *Takes: Stories for Young Adults* (Thistledown Press), which won the Canadian Library Association's Young Adult Award and the Saskatchewan Book Award for Education. She has been three times winner of the Brendon Donnelly Children's Literature Award for Excellence. Debbie Spring lives in Thornhill, Ontario.